Identity Crisis

Laura Scott

Recycling programs for this product may not exist in your area.

LOVE INSPIRED BOOKS

ISBN-13: 978-0-373-67511-1

IDENTITY CRISIS

www.LoveInspiredBooks.com

Printed in U.S.A.

"You're not Mallory, you're Alyssa."

Gage knew he was right. An overwhelming relief washed over him.

"And you know this—how?"

"It's the only thing that makes sense. Earlier you asked me if I believed in God, and I do. So does Alyssa. But Mallory's not a churchgoer. Aly...*you* talked about it."

Slowly she shook her head. "I think you're just saying this to make yourself feel better."

"Feel better about what?" he demanded.

"About how close we came to kissing back there on the sidewalk."

He remembered that moment, when their faces had been close. Too close. "Nothing happened," he denied swiftly. "What's wrong with you? I thought you'd be glad to know your true identity."

"But I don't know my true identity, do I?" she countered. "Telling me I'm Alyssa or Mallory doesn't really change anything. I'm not anyone until I can remember for myself."

He didn't want to admit she was right. While he might be convinced she really was Alyssa, the truth didn't change anything.

She still couldn't remember. Not her identity and not anything related to the danger they were in.

Books by Laura Scott

Love Inspired Suspense

The Thanksgiving Target
Secret Agent Father
The Christmas Rescue
Lawman-in-Charge
Proof of Life
Identity Crisis

LAURA SCOTT

grew up reading faith-based romance books by Grace Livingston Hill, but as much as she loved the stories, she longed for a bit more mystery and suspense. She is honored to write for the Love Inspired Suspense line, where a reader can find a heartwarming journey of faith amid the thrilling danger.

Laura lives with her husband of over twenty-five years and has two children, a daughter and a son, who are both in college. She works as a critical-care nurse during the day at a large level-one trauma center in Milwaukee, Wisconsin, and spends her spare time writing romance.

Please visit Laura at www.laurascottbooks.com, as she loves to hear from her readers.

All the prophets testify about him,
that everyone who believes in him
receives forgiveness of sins through his name.
—*Acts* 10:43

This book is dedicated to my wonderful in-laws Ted and Pat Iding, who welcomed me into their family twenty-seven years ago and have loved me like a daughter. Thanks for always being there.

ONE

Alyssa Roth pulled the hood of her sweatshirt up to cover her newly cropped blond hair as she cautiously approached her town house. She couldn't imagine why her twin sister might have come to her place, but she'd searched all Mallory's usual spots over the past few hours, without success. She'd called and left messages at Mallory's condo and on her cell. She was feeling desperate. She had to find her twin and warn her of the danger.

The hour was close to midnight, so there weren't many people out and about, but that didn't stop her from casting a worried glance over her shoulder. She'd taken a bus from a park-and-ride close to the motel and walked the rest of the way. Using her key, she opened the door and quickly crossed the threshold, locking the door behind her.

The interior was dark so if Mallory was there, she must be sleeping. She pulled a small penlight out of her pocket, unwilling to risk the overhead lights that would effectively broadcast her presence to anyone who might be watching.

Holding the light low at her side, she walked through the kitchen into the living room. She caught an unexpected flash of glitter, and relief washed over her as she realized Mallory's hair clip was on the table beside the sofa.

"Mallory," she whispered loudly as she headed down the hall toward her bedroom. "Wake up. You can't stay here! I'm in danger. I'm being followed and believe it or not, a cop actually tried to kill me!"

There was no response, and when she pushed open the door to her bedroom, her burst of hope faded when she saw the bed was empty. She took two steps into the room before she noticed the dark puddle staining the floor. She stared at it, slowly realizing it was blood.

Too much blood.

Dread sucked the oxygen from her lungs and she stumbled backward, hitting the door frame hard in her effort to get away. What had happened here? Every instinct she possessed screamed at her to run, but she forced herself to stay long enough to sweep her light over the room, half-afraid she'd find Mallory's body. She even went as far as to check the closet and under the bed. Nothing. The only item out of place was a bright yellow blouse, lying crumpled in the far corner, darkly stained with blood.

The hair clip and yellow blouse proved Mallory had been here recently. Alyssa swayed. Nausea threatened to erupt from her stomach in a violent heave. As a nurse, she knew there was too much blood to believe Mallory had escaped unscathed. She stared at the yellow blouse, a sinking realization making her knees weak.

The blouse wasn't Mallory's. It was the blouse she'd bought for herself last week. Her blouse. Her town house. Both full of blood.

She sagged against the door for support as her mind whirled with possibilities. The night before, Councilman Schaefer had gripped her hand and whispered that he'd been stabbed by a hired thug working for Hugh Jefferson. Stunned, she'd gone straight to the authorities, but Officer Crane had brushed aside her concern.

She thought his response was odd, but one minute they were preparing Schaefer for surgery, the next he was dead. Later that night, after her shift at the hospital, a dark blue van tried to run her car off the road and she'd caught a glimpse of Officer Crane's ruddy face before she managed to avoid the crash.

Fearing for her life, she hadn't gone home. She'd checked into a run-down motel and spent the next twelve hours changing her appearance so she looked like Mallory, buying tight clothing and a gaudy purse. She went to the DMV for a new ID and obtained a fake tattoo above her collarbone to match her twin's.

Now she realized her efforts were in vain. She couldn't tear her gaze from the yellow blouse, feeling sick as she realized what must have transpired. Mallory probably had another fight with her ex and had come here to find Alyssa for support. Only, Crane or Jefferson must have been watching her town house and killed Mallory by mistake.

Alyssa was the one who knew how Jefferson had killed Schaefer. She was the one Crane had tried to run off the road. She was the one they wanted to silence.

Not Mallory.

Her fault. Her stomach twisted and she shoved a fist in her mouth to silence the scream building in her chest. This was all her fault. Mallory was the only family she had left in the world. And now her twin was gone. Likely dead. Brutally murdered.

Bands of self-reproach tightened around her throat, squeezing tight. Sheer desperation had forced her to break her cardinal rule by borrowing Mallory's identity. But she shouldn't have rested until she found a way to warn Mallory.

Now it was too late.

Dear Lord, forgive me. Please forgive me!

A shrill whine of police sirens split the night air. Guilt surrendered to fear. She didn't know who had called the police, possibly a neighbor. Had they heard Mallory's scream? She didn't want to think about how her twin must have struggled, fighting for her life. With an effort, she focused on the present. She had to get out of there. Now. She couldn't trust anyone. Especially not the police.

Run! Run! One last glance over her shoulder at the blood-stained blouse ripped her heart in two. She didn't want to leave. But nothing good would come of staying here. She imagined if Mallory was here, her sister would be shouting at her to run. *Don't let them find you, Alyssa. Go! Run!*

Tears streamed down her face, blurring her vision. Galvanized by self-preservation, Alyssa clicked off the penlight and ran down the hall, through the open kitchen and living area, pausing only long enough to snatch the glittery hair clip from the table, stuffing it in her purse as she headed to the front door. Her hand clutched the doorknob. She paused, her heart thundering in her chest. The sirens grew louder. Closer. Too close. The back door?

Spinning on her heel, she retraced her steps, crossing the room toward the kitchen door. She stumbled against the table, unable to see. She swiped at her tears, finally finding the door. Sirens continued to echo outside. Did the police know she was here? Was Officer Crane right now trying to find her?

She left the town house, sprinting into the darkness. The windows in her neighbor's houses were dark—no one was up this late. So who'd called the police? Frantic, she stopped between buildings, trying to think. Indecision held her captive. Finally she ran to the right, through the darkness of her neighbor's backyard.

She ran as fast as she dared. Her heart thundered in her ears. Panic swelled, choking her. The need to move quietly battled a savage desperation to put as much distance between her and the bloody town house as possible.

Don't stop. Don't let them find you. Run!

Where should she go? What should she do? Whom should she trust?

Gage. She needed to find Gage. Her ex-fiancé hadn't believed her when she'd claimed Hugh Jefferson was dangerous. She didn't know why Jefferson had killed Schaefer, but she was convinced everything was related to the hotly contested condos Gage had been hired to build. After Schaefer's claims, she'd called Gage, warned him to stay away from Hugh Jefferson but he'd waved off her concerns. Surely Gage would believe her now. Besides, whom else could she trust?

No one. Only Gage.

She'd broken off their engagement because of Gage's lackluster faith and his overprotective ways. But right now, she longed for his protection, to feel the strength of his arms around her. To bury her face in the safe haven of his chest.

Her breath scissored from her lungs as she ran through alley after alley, backyard after backyard. Shadows in the normally innocuous Milwaukee suburb loomed ominously. She ducked beneath a low-hanging tree branch, its green leaves rustling in the summer night. The sirens went abruptly and eerily silent. Had they arrived at her town house? Did they discover they'd killed the wrong twin? Identical twins didn't have the same fingerprints, so it wouldn't be long before they discovered the truth. Were they out searching for her now? She was too scared to turn around and look.

Dear Lord, help me! Guide me! Keep me safe!

Her breath burned in her chest, threatening to give out for good. She ran for what seemed like forever, but what was probably only thirty to forty minutes. She was in a neighborhood she didn't recognize, but she was too afraid to slow down. The ground beneath her feet abruptly sloped downward. She missed a step. Her ankle twisted sharply under her weight. Pain knifed up her leg. She gasped and fell hard.

The world somersaulted as she rolled down the steep hill, momentum carrying her faster and faster until she smacked bottom. Her skull met the concrete sidewalk with a hard crack. Fireworks of pain exploded in her head.

A velvet shroud of darkness surrounded her.

"Alyssa? Are you there? Pick up the phone!" Gage Drummond scowled as he paused, then added in a calmer tone, "Alyssa, please, *please* call me as soon as you get this message." He flipped the phone shut, hating the feeling of helplessness.

Where was she? The hospital had called him to pick up Mallory because they couldn't reach Alyssa. One of Alyssa's coworkers had assumed he and Alyssa were still engaged and instead of correcting her, he'd agreed to come and get Mallory, hoping to get back into Alyssa's good graces.

Unfortunately, his good deed backfired, because he couldn't get in touch with Alyssa, either. He slipped his phone into his pocket and propped one shoulder against the dingy waiting room wall of Trinity Medical Center's emergency department.

Exhaustion weighed his eyelids. He considered borrowing a cup of the E.D.'s special coma coffee reserved for the graveyard shift. Strong enough to bring you out of a coma, or so Alyssa had claimed.

The memory hurt. He dug his thumbs into his eye sockets in an attempt to ease the pain. Bitter failure coated his tongue. He knew it was his fault she'd left him. But he didn't know how to fix their broken relationship.

Heaving a deep sigh, he opened his eyes and glanced around the waiting room. Surprisingly quiet for a Friday night, or rather early Saturday morning. A homeless man rocked in the corner, keeping a tight hold on his paper sack. One kid within a group of three—all looking like candidates for a Milwaukee gang with spiked hair dyed garish colors and rows of heavy silver chains encircling their necks—held a bloody bandage over his arm. An elderly woman coughed into a tissue and huddled in her seat, as far from the gang wannabes as she could get.

Gage ground his teeth together, detesting the idea of Alyssa working in this place every day. Shortly after she'd agreed to marry him, a junkie strung out on drugs had swung at her, knocking her to the ground and nearly breaking her jaw. He'd been appalled and angry—but even then, she'd refused to quit. Despite some serious arm-twisting on his part. He'd wanted her to stay home, to be safe. Or at the very least, to find a different type of nursing job. What was wrong with working in a nice clinic somewhere? His construction company was doing well enough that he could support both of them, but she wouldn't even discuss the possibility. She'd claimed she liked her job, even the part that required her to care for patients who threatened to harm her.

Gage willed the painful memories away. He was here because he needed to find a way to win Alyssa back. Getting up at two-thirty in the morning and picking up Mallory after her accident should win him some extra credit points, right?

"Gage?" Jennifer, the nurse who'd thought he and Alyssa were still engaged, poked her head into the waiting room. "You can see Mallory now."

Relieved to put the depressing sight of the waiting room behind him, he straightened and followed Jennifer into the arena, an open area surrounded by cubicles. His steel-toed construction boots clunked loudly against the shiny linoleum floor. A sweeping glance at the various employees clustered around the center workstation made him wonder if any of them knew where Alyssa might be. He frowned. He'd dialed her town house at least twenty times since the hospital called. Why hadn't she answered?

Another man? Gage stumbled, managing to catch himself even though his gut twisted painfully. Logically, he knew Alyssa's personal life wasn't any of his business, since she'd broken off their engagement two months ago. A spear of pain stabbed his heart. When she'd given him the ring back, Alyssa's reasons were that he was too over-protective and that he didn't have a close relationship with God. He couldn't figure out what she'd meant. After all, he'd done everything she'd asked of him.

He went to church with her, hadn't he? And he'd joined her Bible study group. It wasn't his fault that he had to work late, missing most of the sessions. He owned his own business and couldn't just switch shifts to get off work the way she did.

After she'd walked out, he'd wondered if maybe the basic truth was simply that Alyssa hadn't loved him. A possibility that had hurt, more than he'd ever imagined it could.

He scowled, pushing the pain aside, and walked into the doorway of the small cubicle. His gaze rested on his ex-fiancée's twin sister. He didn't particularly care for Mallory. She was so completely different from Alyssa. But since she was Alyssa's sister, he made an effort.

"Hey, Mallory," he greeted her with forced politeness. "What happened? How are you feeling?"

She opened her eyes and turned her head toward him. A square white bandage partially covered a large abrasion on her forehead. Gage sucked in a quick breath; the physical resemblance shouldn't have caught him off guard, but it did. Mallory's blond hair was shoulder length and wavy, whereas Alyssa wore hers much longer and straight. Blue eyes, identical to Alyssa's, stared suspiciously into his.

He'd subtly avoided his fiancée's twin because he hadn't appreciated the way Mallory had flirted with him before they'd gotten engaged. Alyssa had brushed it off as Mallory's way of protecting her twin, making sure he would be true to Alyssa, but he didn't buy that theory. He suspected Mallory either wanted to get rid of him, because she was jealous of his relationship with Alyssa, or that she'd wanted to steal him away for herself.

He could have saved her the trouble, because despite their broken engagement, his heart belonged to Alyssa.

Mallory was completely different from Alyssa in too many ways to count. Alyssa upheld her Christian beliefs in everything she said and did, including her stubborn dedication to her career as a trauma nurse. Mallory, on the other hand, was outgoing, known to be the life of the party and an outrageous flirt.

Both women were beautiful on the outside, but in his opinion, only Alyssa had the same beauty deep within. Mallory's personality held a hard edge, whereas Alyssa's was softly inviting.

He missed Alyssa. Desperately. He tried not to dwell on the past, but it wasn't easy. Mallory wordlessly glared at him with distinct annoyance. The corner of her hospital gown slipped off to the side, providing him a distasteful glimpse of the rose and dagger tattoo she wore just below her collarbone.

He quickly averted his gaze, wishing he could just leave. But his job was to get Mallory home. Surely he could manage something so simple.

"Are you ready?" he asked with forced brightness. "I think you're about to be released, so let's bust out of here." There was no sign of the nurse, Jennifer. Where had she gone? To get the discharge paperwork, he hoped. Reluctantly, he tucked his hands in the back pockets of his jeans as he slowly approached Mallory's bedside.

She bolted upright like a shot, bringing up a hand as if to keep him at bay. "Hold it! Who are you? You don't work here." Her suspicious gaze sliced him. "Get out!"

Get out? Was she kidding? He ignored the tiny hairs on the back of his neck that rose in alarm. "Yeah. Very funny."

"This isn't one bit funny." She tugged her gown higher over her chest but thrust her chin in the direction of the door. "I told you to get out."

Gage held out his hands in mock surrender. "You're upset about being stuck with me? Well, too bad. They called me because you have a concussion and can't drive. If I leave, how are you going to get home?"

For a long moment she stared at him, as if he were an alien creature she needed to dissect with X-ray vision. "Home?"

"Yes. Home." He sighed, desperately seeking patience. "To your fancy downtown condo. The sooner I can drop you off, the sooner you'll be rid of me." And then his good deed for the day would be finished.

She reached up with one hand and massaged her temple. "I can't— Let's try this again." Dropping her hand, she leveled a look at him full of uncertainty. "Who are you?"

He stared at her in suspicious shock. Was this some sort of weird game? If so, he wasn't in the mood. He'd already spent his entire evening solving problems at three of his construction sites and had gotten less than four hours of sleep. No way was he doing this.

"Fine. You don't want me to take you home? Then I'm outta here." He spun on his heel but Jennifer walked into the room, blocking his escape route.

"Mallory?" The nurse glanced past him but didn't move from the door. "Dr. Anderson is writing your discharge note as we speak. Would you like to get dressed?"

"No. I want to know what's going on." The tone of her voice held a note of desperation. "Who is this guy? My head hurts. You're telling me to go home, but where is home? Why can't I remember anything?"

Dumbfounded, Gage swiveled toward her. Mallory's confused-yet-defiant gaze met his without an ounce of recognition. Doubt assailed him. Could she honestly be telling the truth?

The nurse was taken aback by Mallory's questions, too. "Since when can't you remember? You didn't say anything when Dr. Anderson examined you."

Mallory massaged her temple again, wincing beneath the pressure of her fingers. "I can't think straight with this headache." She frowned, picking at one corner of the blanket covering her. "It wasn't until this guy mentioned going home that I realized I couldn't remember."

Gage sighed and dropped heavily into a chair beside her bed. Thoughts of returning home for sleep anytime soon faded faster than an early-morning mist. What was going on? Was it possible Mallory really couldn't remember anything?

Jennifer clearly thought so. "I better find Dr. Anderson."

Unfortunately, the doctor didn't have any more

advice to give them. He examined Mallory again, asking a barrage of questions. She knew which year it was and the president of the United States, but not anything personal about herself.

"What's your address?"

"I don't know." Mallory closed her eyes in frustration. Knuckles white, her fists clenched the sheets. She sucked in a loud breath. "I don't understand. What is wrong with me? How can I forget my address?"

"Do you remember any members of your family?" the doctor persisted.

"No." She lifted her shoulder in a shrug. "But I could be an only child."

Gage nearly laughed until he realized she was serious. An only child? Mallory and Alyssa were close, despite their completely different personalities. How could she forget her twin sister?

"Hmm." The doctor frowned and tabbed through the computer screens, reviewing parts of Mallory's electronic medical chart. "There aren't many details regarding your accident. You were found lying on a concrete sidewalk by a neighbor who was coming home after work. Your purse contained some cash and an ID, so we don't really believe this was a mugging. And certainly nothing to indicate a cause for amnesia."

"What do you mean nothing to indicate a cause

for her amnesia?" Gage straightened—his interest piqued, in spite of himself.

The doctor shrugged. "Retrograde amnesia is often the result of a traumatic event combined with a head injury. Mallory has some short-term memory still intact, which even more strongly indicates a traumatic psychological event. However, without knowing what the source of the potential trauma could be, there really isn't anything we can do. We've already performed a CT scan of her head and didn't find any bleeding. When her brain can handle her memory, I'm sure it will return."

Gage rubbed a hand across the back of his neck. "So now what? Does she need to stay here? Get more tests?"

"No, that's not necessary. We've ruled out a head bleed. More tests aren't going to give any input into the source of her amnesia. I'd recommend she be released home, with instructions to follow up with her primary-care doctor in a week. But she really shouldn't be left alone. At least, not until her memory begins to return."

"I'm sure her sister will keep her company." Gage sighed again. Once he managed to find her.

He hoped, prayed, Alyssa hadn't found someone new. Someone from her church, who went to every single Bible study group meeting no matter what.

Someone who may have already replaced him in her heart.

"Good. We'll finish that discharge paperwork."

Gage fell silent after the doctor left the room. He was surprised to find he felt sorry for Mallory. In her current, injured state, he found her less irritating. Although the situation frustrated him to no end. Where was Alyssa?

"A sister? I have a sister?"

He lifted his gaze to meet her abruptly hopeful one. His annoyance faded a bit. "Yeah. Your parents are gone, but you do have a sister. Alyssa is your twin and she's an amazing person."

Mallory's gaze turned curious. "Wow. Sounds like you care about her."

"Yes, I do. Very much," he answered honestly.

"Alyssa." She repeated the name, wrinkling her forehead in concentration. "It's so *wrong* not to remember a twin sister. But the name seems right. Mallory and Alyssa. We're close?"

"Yes, you're close," Gage admitted, because it was true. Despite their differences, the twins always stood by each other no matter what.

"Where is she?" Mallory looked perplexed. "If we're close, why isn't she here?"

"Good question." He reached for his cell phone and redialed. After several long rings there was no answer. He didn't bother leaving another message.

"We'll have to stop over there tomorrow. For now, we'll go back to your place. I'll sleep on the sofa."

"The sofa?" Her blue eyes, so much like Alyssa's, widened in horror. "I'd rather you slept in your car. What part of this don't you understand? I don't know you!"

Her barely restrained annoyance gave more credence to her story than anything else could have. She looked at him as if she detested the sight of him. And maybe she did. He couldn't figure Mallory out. Had never really wanted to.

With a frown, Gage stood. Mallory was more tolerable with amnesia, but he still longed to drop her off as soon as possible. Unfortunately, he was stuck with her until he could find her twin.

So where on earth was Alyssa?

TWO

Even after the hospital staff finally left her alone, she couldn't relax. Her pulse skipped erratically in her chest. Panic clawed up and over her back. Why couldn't she remember?

She fought for control against the invisible demons that snarled in her mind, holding her memory hostage. Logic told her she was in the hospital, but nothing looked familiar. The room was little more than a cubicle, three walls but no real door, just a privacy curtain drawn across the opening. She clutched the blanket tighter. She felt exposed. The flimsy curtain wouldn't protect her. Anyone could come in at any time. *Anyone.*

Like the tall, ruggedly handsome stranger waiting to take her home.

Run! Run! The urge to flee merged with panic. Something was wrong. Very, very, wrong. Certainty seeped into her bones, injecting her with the strength to move. She scrambled from the bed, wincing as her swollen and sprained ankle zinged when her foot hit the floor, and reached for her clothes. Maybe she didn't feel entirely safe around the large, sandy-haired man with the square jaw and golden-brown eyes, but she wasn't afraid of him, either. She grasped the slight distinction eagerly.

Her mind felt as if she were swimming through fog with no shore in sight. She pulled on her jeans, pausing when she noticed two small dark stains. Dried blood? From her head? She put a hand to the bruise above her forehead. No. Her throat closed and she gagged. From someone else. She wildly kicked the jeans off, chest heaving from the effort, pain searing her ankle. The denim landed halfway across the room. Frantic, she rifled through the linens on the cart next to the bed. What could she wear? Scrubs maybe?

"Are you ready?" The deep male voice from the other side of the curtain startled her. She stumbled against the bed, clumsily covering herself with the blanket from the bed.

"No! Stay out!" She stayed where she was until convinced he wasn't coming in. Closing her eyes, she took several deep breaths, fighting a wave of dizziness. *Come on, get a grip.* Steeling her resolve, she forced herself to limp across the room to fetch the dreaded clothes. With an effort she donned the midriff-baring T-shirt and hip-hugging jeans.

The name Mallory seemed right but the clothes felt foreign. Wearing such tightly fitting jeans and T-shirt was embarrassing. Why did she wear them? Didn't she care if others stared? Mallory gave her head a shake, and then winced as the pickax hammering in her head intensified.

This wasn't the time to worry about her clothes. Focus. She needed to focus. Urgency propelled her forward. With a suppressed shiver she pulled on the lightweight denim jacket. The bottom of the jacket barely met the waistband on her jeans. She tugged on it, as if she could will it longer, and then gave up. Close enough.

She picked up the huge, gaudy purse, slung it over her shoulder and yanked the curtain aside with a snap. "I'm ready. Let's go."

His gaze raked over her and she fought the urge to tug once more on the short hem of her T-shirt. His amber eyes held no clue to his thoughts. "Great."

He led the way through the emergency room, keeping his pace slow so she could keep up with her bum ankle. She swept a glance over the occupants of the waiting room, her attention snagged by a hacking cough. Despite her desire to leave as quickly as possible, her steps slowed to a stop.

An elderly woman sat huddled in a corner, her lips as blue as her hair. Mallory abruptly changed course, heading toward the woman, who held a crumpled, blood-stained tissue in the palm of her hand. The poor woman looked as if she was ready to take her last breath.

"Get a doctor over here, now!" Mallory called out to a passing nurse. "This woman's on the verge of respiratory arrest."

The harried nurse sputtered an argument but then noticed the same bluish tinge to the woman's lips that had drawn Mallory's attention. "I'll get an oxygen tank."

Seconds later, the nurse hurried over wheeling an oxygen tank. She cranked up the dial and placed an oxygen mask over the elderly woman's face. "Take a deep breath, Mrs. Sullivan. We're going to get you into a room right now." The nurse touched a button on a device hanging from a lanyard around her neck that must have functioned like some sort of intercom. "Steve, I need a wheelchair brought into the waiting room, stat."

Mallory watched as one of the orderlies brought over a wheelchair. Soon, the elderly woman was escorted back. Satisfied, she turned back toward the entrance.

Only to find the tall stranger staring at her in shocked surprise. "What was that about?"

"What do you mean?"

"How did you know she was going into respiratory arrest?" His gaze was suspicious and faintly accusing.

Good question. How had she known? "I'm not sure."

He stared at her again, seemingly at a loss for words. She couldn't understand his reaction, especially when he abruptly turned and continued walking through the door.

She quickened her gimpy pace, following him through the doors to the parking lot. "Wait! I can't move that fast!"

He spun around and came back toward her, his face pulled into a grimace. "Sorry," he muttered, although somehow she suspected that deep down he really wasn't.

Mallory didn't know why she annoyed him, but worse, she couldn't remember his name. Had he even told her? She couldn't remember. Her head hurt so badly she could barely concentrate.

And suddenly, the nearly invisible thread of control snapped. "Look, Mr. Whatever-Your-Name is, I don't know what your problem is and I don't care. Have you forgotten your promise to take me home?

Or are you going to leave me stranded here without a ride?"

"I said I'm sorry. I shouldn't have snapped at you like that." He scrubbed a hand over his face, and she couldn't help noticing the deep grooves of fatigue bracketing the sides of his mouth. Maybe it wasn't personal. Maybe he was just tired. "Don't worry, I won't leave you stranded."

He seemed to be making an effort to remain calm, adjusting his stride to meet hers, as they headed across the parking lot. He opened the door of a pickup truck and gestured for her to get in. Her tight jeans hindered her movement as she tried to jump into the truck seat.

"Do you need help?"

"No." Her cheeks burned with embarrassment as she struggled to leverage herself up and into the truck. He waited patiently then closed the door gently but firmly once she was safely inside.

She let out a tiny breath of relief when he climbed in beside her. She couldn't explain why she wanted to get away from the hospital, but the need to escape couldn't be ignored. She placed her palms on her thighs, trying to hide the bloodstains. If he saw them, he'd have questions, and unfortunately she didn't have any answers.

She wished more than anything that she didn't have to depend on him to take her home. His shoulders strained at the seams of his white cotton shirt as he started the truck and pulled out of the parking lot. The cuffs of his sleeves were rolled to his elbows. Dark hair sprinkled his skin. She fought the absurd urge to touch him.

"Gage."

She tore her glance from the mesmerizing strength of his arms. "Excuse me?"

"My name is Gage Drummond. Alyssa and I are—close friends."

Mallory lobbed the name through the spacious portion of her brain where her memory should have been. Gage was a nice name. "Yes. So you said."

He kept his eyes glued to the road. "Alyssa is a nurse. She works in the emergency department of Trinity Medical Center."

"I see." Mallory filed away that small tidbit of information. She had a twin sister who was a nurse and her boyfriend's name was Gage. Comforting, to a certain extent, to know she wasn't completely alone in the world. "Am I a nurse, too?"

"No." His response was terse. "You're an interior designer, working for a large architectural firm. You create color schemes for offices, hospitals, that sort of thing. So don't you think it's odd that you knew that woman was about to go into respiratory arrest?"

"Her lips were blue," she said, even though a

blanket of unease settled over her, worse than the one she'd felt earlier when she'd woken up in the hospital with a fog-filled brain. The minute she'd noticed the elderly woman in the corner, she'd known something was wrong. Respiratory arrest was when someone stopped breathing. Despite Gage's claim she was a designer, she must have had some exposure to hospitals. Maybe she'd tried to follow her sister into nursing, but then dropped out? Why on earth couldn't she remember? Mallory licked suddenly dry lips and tried to shrug. "Everyone knows blue lips are a bad sign."

Gage's laugh didn't hold any mirth. "Yeah, maybe. Or this is part of some weird way of changing yourself into someone I'd like. Don't bother trying to flirt with me again. I happen to love Alyssa."

Mallory gaped at him in shock. "What are you talking about?" His comment floored her. Why would she try to flirt with him? Before he became involved with Alyssa? Or after? She felt a little sick that she might have treated her sister that way.

"Never mind," he said, as if he regretted bringing the subject up in the first place.

Ignoring the pounding in her head, she lifted her chin. "Rest assured I'm not interested in flirting with you."

"Good."

Silence hung heavy between them. Mallory shifted her attention to the scenery outside her window, at least the part she could see through the darkness. Arguing with the stranger had temporarily held fear at bay, but without something to occupy her brain, the sense of doom clung, lining her clothes, abrading her skin.

The night swallowed them, yet she felt safer inside the truck next to Gage than she had inside the busy, well-lit emergency department. Why? Why did she feel safer with a stranger? Peering through the window, she sought the source of her earlier apprehension. Was someone out there, looking for her? Whose blood stained her clothes?

Her blank memory didn't supply any answers. Outside, there was the faintest hue of light near the horizon, telling her dawn wasn't too far off. Yet dozens of stars still littered the sky. Leafy green trees and mild temperatures told her the season was summer. The seemingly calm and peaceful landscape was at odds with her inner angst.

Where, exactly, were they? Why wouldn't this haze over her mind go away? She focused on several street signs, seeking even one that seemed familiar. All the while, she was keenly aware of the stranger's disapproving presence beside her.

Not a stranger. Gage. Gage Drummond. She forced herself to use his name. They weren't strangers just because she couldn't remember him. He obviously knew her, at least enough to offer a ride in the middle of the night. But enough to protect her from harm? That she wasn't sure of. How could she have tried to flirt with him?

She risked a glance at him from beneath her lashes. There was no denying Gage was a very attractive man. Obviously, her sister was a very lucky woman. Her gaze clung to his hand, so strong, so capable on the steering wheel. His arms were firmly muscled and tan as if he spent a lot of time in the sun. She clenched her hands in her lap to keep from reaching out to touch him.

Gage and Alyssa were close, but where was Alyssa now? She found it odd how he didn't seem to have a clue where to find her. How often did a guy lose his girlfriend? Maybe he wasn't being entirely truthful. Maybe her sister's relationship with this man was on the rocks. Mallory swallowed hard. Harboring a secret attraction for her sister's boyfriend made her a horrible sister. She had to stop thinking about him, right now. So what if Gage exuded a confident strength she was drawn to? A strength she longed to lean upon?

Gage wasn't anything to her. She didn't even remember him. Rocky relationship or not, he belonged to Alyssa. Besides, he couldn't have made his feelings toward her more clear.

Forget about him. Even if Gage didn't know where her sister was, his feelings were obviously tangled into knots over it. And since she was dependent on him, she decided it was time to make amends. "I'm sorry."

"For what?"

"For whatever I did to put a wedge between you and Alyssa."

He was quiet for a long moment. "There is no wedge between me and Alyssa. And Mallory doesn't apologize. Ever."

She didn't need her memory to know she couldn't win this one. She threw her hand up then lightly tapped the side of her temple. "Silly me, I forgot." Sarcasm dripped from her words. "Consider my apology rescinded."

A few minutes later, Gage pulled up in front of a fancy-looking building in the heart of the city. She tensed and stared. Was this some sort of test? Did she really live here?

"Where are we?" She hated having to ask.

"Your place. Do you have your keys?" Gage asked, pausing in the act of opening his door.

"No. I meant what city?"

"Milwaukee, Wisconsin." He held out his hand patiently. "I need your keys."

Milwaukee didn't sound dangerous, but the sense of urgency wouldn't leave her alone. Mallory pulled open her large, gaudy purse and searched for the keys. She'd already gone through her wallet and found the pitiful amount of cash and her driver's license. There was also a package of tissues, a glittery hair clip, enough cosmetics to stock several counters at the department store and a hairbrush. No cell phone, which she thought odd. Why wouldn't she have a cell phone? Finally, her fingers closed around a ring of keys. Feeling relieved, she pulled them out and dangled them in front of him.

Gage grabbed them and jumped out of the truck. She slid out of the passenger side, favoring her ankle as she landed on the sidewalk. She followed him, moving at a much slower pace. The back of her neck tingled when she watched him use her key to gain access to the secured building. He held the door open for her, and Mallory felt admiration for his polite gestures. But before she crossed the threshold, she couldn't resist a furtive glance over her shoulder. No one lurked behind them. At least not that she could see.

But she kept wondering if someone was out there. Following her. Watching her.

Trying to control a flash of anxiety, she turned her attention to the building where she lived. The place was fancy, all chrome and glass with a decor that reeked of money. Had she designed the color scheme for this building? She guessed the condos inside were not of the traditional postage-stamp variety.

Gage waited, one strong arm holding open the elevator door for her. The elevator was surrounded by glass windows, providing a breathtaking view of the city lights. Yet she couldn't help feeling exposed, knowing that anyone outside could easily see them standing inside.

She tried to ignore the increasing paranoia. Was that a common reaction for people who had amnesia? Maybe.

When Gage reached over and pushed the button for the fifteenth floor, she was hit by a sense of familiarity. As if she'd done the same thing herself.

Her head ached with the strain of trying to remember. The sense of urgency grew stronger, and she tapped her foot as the elevator slid upward. The flashes of familiarity were encouraging. Maybe her memory would return after she'd gotten into more familiar surroundings. When the elevator doors opened on the fifteenth floor, she eagerly stepped out.

Oddly enough, there was only one door. Did she live in some sort of penthouse? Silently he used her key to gain access. Warily she stepped inside. The condo was huge, decorated with red furniture, black and red kitchen cabinets and white walls.

Large windows lined one entire wall, giving her a breathtaking view of Lake Michigan.

"Wow." Drawn by the cool, calm water, where the sun was just beginning to creep up the horizon, she hobbled to the window. The lake was a balm to her frayed nerves. "I have spectacular taste," she murmured, impressed with the view.

Gage grunted, hovering in the entrance, as if uncomfortable in her private space. "You obviously like a lot of bold colors."

Bold colors were an understatement. She wasn't about to admit that the deep red, blue and black interior had almost made her wrinkle her nose in distaste. She must have liked the furnishings at some point in time. She swept a gaze over the room, noting a short hallway off to the left where she assumed her bedroom and bathroom were located.

"Have anything to drink around here?" Gage asked.

She glanced at him, raising a brow. "How would I know? I'll have to look."

When she limped in the direction of her kitchen, he frowned and glanced at her swollen ankle as if he could tell the pain was getting worse with each step. "Stay put, you should rest that ankle. I'll do it." He walked toward the fridge and opened the door. She paused, nearly shedding her jacket but then swiftly reconsidering, remembering the mid-riff-baring T-shirt. Better to stay covered up.

Feeling awkward in her own surroundings, she watched as Gage rummaged around and finally withdrew a jug of orange juice.

"Want some?" He held the container and two glasses. The expression on his face was carefully polite. His cinnamon-colored eyes looked directly into hers.

She dragged her gaze away with an effort. "Sure. I need to take the anti-inflammatory that the doctor prescribed." She pulled the pill bottle out of her purse. "He assured me it's only a sprain, but my ankle really hurts."

The inane conversation didn't bring the normalcy she desired. She was home, but something was wrong, she could feel it in her bones. There was nothing homey about this condo. Frankly, she couldn't imagine living there.

He poured her a glass of juice and she stepped closer, wary of invading his space. Silly, considering they were in her condo. She tossed the pills back and quickly took a sip of juice. The cool liquid soothed her parched throat.

"Anything look familiar?" Gage cocked an eyebrow over the rim of his glass.

"No." She downed the rest of the juice in a big gulp then set the glass down with a thud. The condo should be a safe haven, but a strong sense of disquiet kept her off balance. She fingered the bloodstains on her jeans and then wrapped her arms around her body, warding off a chill.

What would Gage say if she wrapped her arms around his lean waist, asking him to hold her? He was a stranger, but so far he was the only person who made her feel safe. The condo wasn't much better than the hospital. Would she ever feel safe again? She glanced at Gage, noted the restlessness in his eyes. She didn't want him to leave, yet he just as clearly didn't want to stick around.

For a moment panic surged at the thought of being left here alone. She reached out to touch his arm, a solid anchor for her shaky, trembling foundation. "Gage—"

A sizzle of awareness leaped between them. Gage jerked from her touch, sending a wave of juice sloshing to the floor.

Mallory snatched her hand away, her fingers tingling from the solid warmth of his skin.

"I have to go. I'll check on you later." Gage hastily set his half-full glass down on the counter. Stepping over the mess, he gave her a wide berth as he headed for the door.

Mallory couldn't think of a single thing to say as he left the condo. She didn't understand the urge to beg him not to go. He might be a close *friend* of her twin, but he was still a stranger. Her knees gave way as she sank onto the nearest chair. Loneliness surrounded her, magnifying her dread.

She didn't want to stay here, but where could she go? What could she do? Run after Gage? Beg him to take her home with him? Throw herself into his arms?

She buried her face in her hands, full of self-loathing. What kind of person was she? And what sort of mess had she gotten herself into?

Gage's hands shook, making it difficult to slide the truck key into the ignition. Finally he jammed the metal home and started the truck with a twist of his wrist. He floored the accelerator, speeding away from Mallory's high-rise condo as if his life depended on putting distance between them.

His heart nearly hammered its way out of his chest. What was wrong with him? He must have accidently touched Mallory a dozen times in passing and never once experienced the jolt of electricity like the one that just zapped him. He rubbed a shaky hand over the stubble on his chin. He must be losing his mind. Alyssa was the twin he was attracted to. Not Mallory.

Calmer now, he realized he'd reacted that way only because he missed Alyssa. She'd broken things off, but he wanted to win her back. Somehow he'd transposed his feelings for Alyssa onto Mallory. Because Mallory with amnesia wasn't acting like Mallory. Twisted logic? Maybe. But he couldn't come up with anything else that made sense.

For a moment he wondered if Alyssa and Mallory had switched places. Was it possible the woman he'd just dropped off was really Alyssa? His chest filled with hope, but then he slowly shook his head. No way. He refused to believe it. Alyssa told him she and Mallory had vowed to never switch identities. And Alyssa always told the truth.

He couldn't imagine any circumstance where Alyssa would agree to take Mallory's place. More likely, Mallory's strange actions arose from some identity crisis, a direct result of her amnesia. And why did he care? Mallory's amnesia wasn't his problem anymore. His good deed was finished.

She was Alyssa's problem now. He didn't head home but hooked a left turn toward Alyssa's town house. It was early, five-thirty in the morning, but that didn't stop him.

Shortly after their engagement, she'd given him a key to keep as a spare and he'd been remiss in returning it, hoping they'd get back together so he wouldn't need to. Since their split they'd spoken on occasion, civil conversations that had done nothing to fix the true problems between them.

On her front porch, he took a deep breath and lifted his hand to knock. She didn't answer, so he tried one more time to call her cell phone. Still no answer.

Steeling his resolve, he tried the door handle, oddly reassured to find the door locked. Alyssa always locked the door when she was gone. Using the key, he unlocked the door and pushed it open.

The heavy scent of pine cleaner layered with ammonia assaulted his senses. With a frown, he flipped on a switch, flooding the foyer with light. "Alyssa?" His voice reverberated loudly through the room. He stepped over the threshold, shutting the door behind him.

Her town house was always impeccably neat and clean, but the thick scent of the cleaner nearly choked him. It was as if the entire place had been doused in the stuff, which was odd, since Alyssa normally used vinegar to clean because it was better for the environment. He poked his head into the kitchen and living room, finding them both empty. The windows were all closed, but the air-conditioning wasn't turned on. Alyssa preferred fresh air from open windows, especially in the summer. Gage forced himself to walk down the hall, his footsteps echoing loudly on the hardwood floor. The pine scent mixed with ammonia grew impossibly stronger.

Her bedroom door hung partially open. Holding his breath, he pushed it the rest of the way until he could see her bed, neatly made. Discovering she wasn't home didn't sit well with him.

Where could she be? He knew Alyssa's Christian values wouldn't allow her to spend the night with a man. And if she wasn't with Mallory, or at work, where could she be?

The ammonia scent made his head hurt, so he opened the windows as he walked back through her town house. A sick feeling settled in his gut. Something wasn't right. Maybe he should call Jonah Stewart. His childhood friend was a detective with the Milwaukee police, and he had connections that would help in looking for Alyssa. But how long had she been gone?

She might not be missing at all. For all he knew, she was with some nursing friends from work. Or visiting a sick friend. He decided to wait here in the town house for her. Surely she'd come home sooner or later.

In the kitchen, the blinking light of the answering machine snagged his gaze. His messages to her would be on there, but what if there were others? A clue to her whereabouts?

Ignoring a flash of guilt, Gage rewound the tape and hit the play button. The first message came through almost immediately.

"Alyssa, this is Kristine from Trinity Medical Center. You requested a two-week personal leave of absence. You know the summer is our busiest time of the year because of increase in trauma patients, but since you sounded desperate, we've agreed to grant your leave."

Stunned, Gage hit the stop button on the machine. A two-week leave of absence? Why in the world would Alyssa desperately need two weeks off? The only family she had left was her sister, Mallory.

Maybe there really was a sick friend somewhere.

He hit the play button again. Aside from the messages he'd left, there were no other messages. Not even one from Mallory.

Gage turned away from the machine. Idly, he opened her fridge. The contents were spartan, no milk or anything that would spoil. Butter, ketchup and mustard, along with a jug of water, were left inside. He closed the door.

The house had been closed up tight and there was nothing to eat. Where had Alyssa gone? The last time he'd spoken to her was just two days ago when she'd called him from work, anxious to get together. Idiot that he was, he'd been thrilled by the idea that she'd wanted a chance to mend their relationship. Then she'd mentioned having grave concerns over his taking on the Jefferson condo project. She knew his construction company had been awarded the contract to build the new Riverside Luxury Condos owned by Hugh Jefferson. Condos that had been hotly debated within the city government for well over a year. She claimed there was something dangerous going on, and she begged him to cancel the contract.

He'd scoffed at her concern. First of all, he needed that contract. And besides, what could be so bad about building condos overlooking the Milwaukee River? The idea was ludicrous.

Until now. Alyssa's empty town house caused tension to slither like a snake through his belly. He didn't have any concrete reason to believe she was in danger, but the persistent worry wouldn't quit. Had something happened to her? Had he failed, again? The image of his dead mother swam in his mind and he shoved it away with effort.

Failure wasn't an option. Not this time. Because he knew his heart and soul wouldn't survive if he failed to find and protect Alyssa.

THREE

Since leaving wasn't an option, Mallory restlessly limped around her penthouse condo, searching for clues to jar her memory. Oddly, there wasn't an overabundance of personal items lying around. She discovered she had an eclectic taste in music ranging from rap to jazz. Several new-wave art prints were splashed on her walls. Nice, but she couldn't shake the awful feeling she was looking at her things through a stranger's eyes.

Bone-weary, she fought off an encroaching wave of fatigue. She blinked and forced her eyes to stay open. There had to be something here that could make her remember who she was. Or why she continued to feel an overwhelming sense of doom. Hoping to find more personal items, she headed down the hall, toward the bedroom.

On the dresser she found a framed snapshot of her and Alyssa. She picked up the photo, surprised to realize just how much they looked alike physically. Alyssa was easy to identify, since she was conservatively dressed and wore her long blond hair pulled back in a French braid. Alyssa's expression was full of joy, and she proudly wore a modest diamond on the third finger of her left hand.

In contrast, Mallory wore a slinky rose-colored dress, and despite the bright smile on her face, there was a certain sadness reflected in her eyes.

Who'd taken their picture? A man? Gage?

Mallory set the photo down with a grimace. This unhealthy fascination with her sister's boyfriend had to stop. She needed to focus her attention on filling the cavernous blanks in her memory. On searching for the person whose blood stained her jeans.

Alyssa's boyfriend was definitely off-limits.

The huge bed was softly inviting, but she refused to simply go to sleep when she had no idea what was going on. Or why she might be sad in contrast to her sister's happiness.

Her control slipped and suddenly she couldn't stand wearing the uncomfortable and blood-splattered clothes another minute. She stripped everything off as quickly as humanly possible.

After a good hour in the bathroom, scrubbing her skin until it was almost raw, she felt much better. But finding something appropriate and comfortable to wear wasn't easy. She rooted through drawers, searching until she found a clean T-shirt that didn't fit too snuggly and a comfortable pair of yoga pants.

On the opposite side of the bed, a bundle of rose-colored silk on the floor caught her eye. Intrigued, she leaned down and picked up the garment, fingering the fabric thoughtfully. It was a gown, cut daringly low. She had no memory of wearing it, or of leaving it lying crumpled on the floor, as if she'd changed in a hurry. She lifted the dress and glanced around the otherwise neat room. From what she could tell, she wasn't normally a slob.

Had she worn the gown recently? She spread the rose silk on a nearby chair, wishing the simple item of clothing would spark some sort of memory. If not the gown, something else, then? She opened the closet door and rifled through the hanging garments. Only, nothing looked familiar. Her gaze landed on two boxes sitting on the closet floor.

Wincing against the swelling in her ankle, she kneeled beside the boxes and opened the flap of the top one. She found winter clothing, mainly turtlenecks and cashmere sweaters. She shoved that box aside and grabbed the second. This one held more clothes. Men's clothes.

The sick feeling in her stomach intensified as she stared at the contents of the box. Had she lived with someone? Been married? She wasn't wearing a ring. Divorced, then? And if so, from whom? She really should have asked Gage more questions.

Digging beneath the clothes, she found expensive dress shoes and a leather shaving case. Nothing else. Nothing to give a clue as to the identity of the owner.

Dazed, she stumbled to her feet. Limping over to the dresser, she opened every single drawer, relieved to find only female items of clothing. She couldn't explain why the thought that she may have actually lived with a man so bothersome. Except that it didn't seem like something she'd agree to do.

In the bottom drawer, beneath more sweaters— really, how many sweaters did one person need?— she found a buttery-soft, brown suede box.

Expecting to find jewelry, she was surprised to discover it empty except for a glossy photo lying inside. Hesitantly, she picked up the picture.

This time, she was dressed in yet another evening gown, this one in brilliant blue. But she wasn't alone. A man held her possessively in his arms. She swallowed hard, her stomach gurgling with tension as she studied the picture. The guy looked older than her, maybe in his mid- to late thirties, and was dressed in an expensive suit. His handsome face held a note of triumph, but she looked less than thrilled. A faint hint of distaste shadowed her gaze.

Who was he? The owner of the clothing she'd found in the box? Staring at the background behind them, she could see they were standing in some hotel, with linen-covered tables and an orchestra behind them. How many hotels were there in Milwaukee? Or even worse, how many hotels were in the entire United States? No way to know where the photo had been taken.

She put the glossy photo back inside the box, hoping, praying that the men's clothing belonged to some sort of ex-husband rather than just some guy she'd decided to live with. She didn't want to believe she was that sort of woman. But the slinky evening gowns and the revealing clothes, not to mention the rose and dagger tattoo she'd discovered just below her collarbone, told a different story.

She closed her eyes on a wave of helplessness. *Please, Lord, help me remember!*

Loud pounding on her door startled her. She spun from the dresser, nearly falling on her face when her ankle screamed with pain. Her pulse jumped and, despite the T-shirt and yoga pants, she really wanted a robe or something to cover up with.

Since there didn't seem to be anything nearby, she yanked the blanket off the bed and wrapped it around her. Gripping the lower hem of the blanket so she wouldn't trip, she made her way down the hall toward the front door.

The banging grew insistently louder.

Nervously, she peered through the peephole. Gage's face, distorted by the glass, had her sighing in relief.

Not the guy in the photo or some other stranger. Gage. Gage had come back. A wave of pleasure swelled in her chest, and she quickly squelched it. What was wrong with her? He didn't belong to her, he belonged to Alyssa!

"Open up, Mallory," he called.

Hanging on to the blanket with one hand, she opened the door. "How did you get in? Isn't there security here?"

"I accidently kept your keys. And that's not important right now. Finding Alyssa is." He brushed past her, tossing the keys onto the kitchen counter. With a sigh, she closed the door behind him.

"I'm sorry, but I can't help you." The sheer agony on his face made her feel bad, as if she should be doing something more to help. "I'm afraid my memory hasn't returned."

He stared at her as if just noticing her for the first time. "What's with the blanket?"

She flushed and gripped the edges tighter. "I couldn't find a robe."

Gage gave her an odd look but didn't say anything. "Hurry up and get ready. Because we're heading out, together, to find Alyssa."

It was on the tip of her tongue to argue, but in the end, she didn't really want to stay here alone. Going out somewhere, anywhere, would be better than sitting around waiting for her memory to return. "All right, give me a couple of minutes."

"A couple of minutes?" The surprise in his tone made her glance back at him over her shoulder. "I'll hold you to that."

Once again, she tried to find clothing that she wouldn't be embarrassed to wear in public. In the very back of the closet, she found a pair of slacks that weren't skintight, and she gratefully pulled them on. She found a long-sleeved, somewhat sheer blouse and pulled that over the plain T-shirt and buttoned it all the way up, not caring about the lack of fashion. Running shoes were harder to find, but she finally found a pair that looked almost brand-new in the back of the closet.

Odd, how there were parts of her that didn't seem quite right. Did amnesia make a person forget his or her personality? Or maybe a more likely answer was that she put on an act on the outside, hiding her true self within. But why would she put on an act for the public? Because she was afraid? Or because she had something to hide?

Her sister, Alyssa, was the one person who

might know for sure. Mallory grimly realized that she needed to find her twin as much as Gage did, maybe more.

Gage seemed a little surprised when she returned to the living room in less than five minutes, but then he gestured to the answering machine in the corner. "You didn't listen to your messages?"

"No." She didn't want to admit the simple task hadn't occurred to her. "Why?"

He crossed over to press the button on the machine, which was located on the back wall of her kitchen. She followed more slowly, carefully stepping over the sticky orange juice mess she'd left on the floor. She felt foolish having avoided the kitchen after the scene with Gage.

"Mallory? This is Rick Meyer. We won the bid for the Jefferson project. I'd like to get started with some color schemes as soon as possible, so call me." Gage hit the button to stop the tape.

She stared at him. "Who's Rick Meyer?" Was it possible he was the older guy in the photo with her?

"Your boss. But I'm looking for a message from Alyssa." Gage rewound the tape and then replayed all the messages from the beginning.

"Mallory? Call me the second you get this message. It's urgent that we talk as soon as possible."

Gage stopped the machine. "That's her."

Mallory nodded. Her sister's voice sounded like an exact replica of her own. "I figured as much. But what does it mean? Why would it be so urgent that we talk?"

"I don't know." Gage spun away from the counter, his movements agitated. "Alyssa called me two days ago. She sounded paranoid, saying something about the Jefferson project being dangerous. She wanted me to drop the project and warned me to be careful."

Mallory suppressed a shiver. There was no denying the tense note of fear in her sister's tone. The laughing image of Alyssa standing beside her in the photograph mocked her. "What exactly is the Jefferson project?"

Gage dropped into a kitchen chair. "Hugh Jefferson is a wealthy businessman from Chicago. He bought several old warehouse properties along the Milwaukee River and apparently promised to bring in businesses, but then changed his mind and decided to build condos instead. The city government wasn't pleased and fought him tooth and nail, refusing to change the zoning permits. After a year-long debate, Jefferson finally got his permits and my company was awarded the construction contract. Despite the hassle of getting it approved, the project is nothing more than a real-estate endeavor. I can't see how there's anything dangerous about it."

Mallory frowned and sat at the kitchen table across from Gage. She tried to make sense of the pieces, which frankly was easier than trying to remember. "I don't understand. What gave Alyssa the impression it might be dangerous?"

Gage scrubbed his hands over his face. "She worked the trauma room the night City Councilman Ray Schaefer was brought in. Apparently he was mugged and stabbed twice in the abdomen. According to Alyssa, before he died he told her a guy hired by Hugh Jefferson stabbed him."

"He died?" The blood-splattered clothes she'd been wearing flashed in her mind. Logically, she couldn't imagine she'd been anywhere near the councilman who'd died, but then again, the doctor did say that her amnesia was the result of a traumatic event. Watching a man being stabbed certainly would be traumatic. Had she really been there? Was Schaefer the guy standing with her in the photo? Her nausea deepened.

"Yeah, but according to a statement made by the chief of police, Councilman Schaefer was killed in a simple mugging, and they'd already caught the gang member who'd done the crime. The councilman was in the wrong place at the wrong time, and the kid had stabbed him as part of a gang-initiation dare."

So she hadn't been there. Her relief was quickly replaced with fear. "But what if the chief of police is wrong?"

Gage's face reflected his skepticism. "How could he be wrong? They caught the guy—it was all over the news."

"Yet Alyssa sounded frantic and claimed the project was dangerous." She tried to curb the rising panic.

"Thinking the worst isn't going to help." Gage's expression was one of sheer determination. "I have to believe Alyssa is all right. And I have to trust that we're going to find her."

Arguing wouldn't help, so she let the matter drop. Think. She needed to think. "Okay, if Alyssa was worried about something shady going on, what would she do?"

"She tried coming to me." Gage stared down at his hands for a long moment. Self-reproach shimmered from his cinnamon-colored eyes. Sympathy stirred deep in her heart. He really cared about her sister. And the radiant happiness reflected in Alyssa's eyes on the glossy photo was a strong indication she felt the same way about him.

The two of them deserved to find happiness together. She should be thrilled for them. So why did she feel depressed?

Gage raised anguished eyes to hers. "Since I refused to help, I'm not sure what she'd do. I left a message with a friend of mine who might be able to help find her. I checked her place, but she's not there. I even stopped at my house, but she wasn't there, either. All I know for sure is that she called you."

Mallory nearly apologized, before she caught herself. "Okay, obviously Alyssa's not here. Who are Alyssa's closest friends? People from work? Maybe she's staying with one of them because she was afraid to be alone?"

"Yeah. Maybe." Gage brightened, as if he hadn't considered that option. "I think Paige Sanders and Emma Banks are her closest friends from work. We can start with them."

"And what if they're not home, or don't want to talk to us?" She watched as Gage swiftly paged through the phone book.

"We'll find a way to make them talk." He scowled darkly. "Because I'm not leaving until we have answers."

Gage slammed the phone book shut with a sense of frustration. He wasn't close to Alyssa's friends, another thing she'd complained about while they were engaged, and he soon realized he didn't know if either of the women were married, which meant they might not be listed under their own last name in the directory.

Finally he asked Mallory to call Trinity Medical Center, pretending to be Alyssa to request the numbers. He wasn't surprised when she was readily given the information. Mallory sounded more like Alyssa now that she had amnesia than she did before. He tried to put his finger on the difference. Maybe because the brittle edge had vanished from her tone.

Mallory acted more like Alyssa now, too. Not only was the sharp edge gone, but she didn't flirt the way she had before she'd hit her head. Even her clothes were more conservative than usual.

Thankfully, after that fiasco in the kitchen, she'd kept her distance from him. Which was a huge relief.

He felt bad for her. Having amnesia couldn't be easy. His memories of Alyssa were painful, but at least he had them. He couldn't imagine what his life would be like if he couldn't remember Alyssa.

"I have the phone numbers," Mallory said. He gratefully took the slip of paper and then used directory assistance to get addresses. At least they still had home phone numbers, because cell numbers would have been a dead end. Finally they were ready to leave. Hoping Jonah Stewart, his detective friend, would return his call soon, he waited, rather impatiently, while Mallory grabbed her massive purse and slung it over her shoulder.

She must not have noticed his impatience, because she grinned at him. "Okay. I'm ready, Freddie."

For a moment he stared at her in shock. *I'm ready, Freddie,* was a phrase Alyssa had often used, but had he ever heard Mallory say it? He tried to think back but couldn't honestly remember. She sounded too much like Alyssa, which made it harder to remember that he didn't like her. Normally Mallory was easy to dismiss. Especially since he'd already fallen for Alyssa.

He jerked the door open, and then paused to glance back at Mallory. Was it possible that Mallory was really more like Alyssa than he'd ever realized? She'd never acted anything like her twin, until now. "You're sure you don't remember anything?" he couldn't help asking.

"Oh, sure, I'm faking amnesia." She rolled her eyes with exasperation. "Of course I don't remember. Why would I bother to pretend?" Mallory truly looked perplexed.

To be more like Alyssa. To make me like you. Gage bit back the words before they could slip off his tongue. "Never mind. Let's go."

He closed and locked Mallory's door then headed for the glass elevator. He kept his gaze straight ahead. He wasn't particularly fond of heights. But he also refused to cave in to his fear. If anyone on a construction site knew he built tall buildings but was afraid of heights, he'd be the topic of endless jokes. Even on-site, he forced himself to manage every phase of a building project, even if that meant going up to the top.

He was glad when they reached the lobby level. Outside the sun was shining and puffy white clouds dotted the sky, the wind off the lake bringing a gust of cool air. A nice day, but he didn't care. Alyssa was missing and he was stuck with Mallory. He couldn't relax, not until he knew Alyssa was safe.

He glanced at Mallory, surprised when he saw her blue eyes filled with stark apprehension as she glanced around as if she'd never seen this part of the city before.

He'd wanted Mallory to come with him because he thought Alyssa's friends would respond better to her twin. He could only assume Alyssa had told her closest friends how they'd broken up. He and Alyssa had known each other for only about three months before getting engaged, and they'd tended to keep to themselves. He had no idea what reason Alyssa had given her friends for breaking off their engagement, but he suspected Alyssa confided that he was the problem.

Mallory stopped in the middle of the sidewalk, forcing another couple to step around her. Lost in thoughts of Alyssa, Gage followed too close and smacked his chin on her head.

"Ow." She rubbed the top of her head. He hastily backed up, putting at least a foot of space between them. "This is so frustrating. I'm walking along like I should know where we're going, but I don't."

"Over there." Gage nodded toward his truck, parked a few car lengths down the street. "The blue pickup."

"What about the rest of them?" She waited for several pedestrians to pass by before gesturing toward the scattered cars parked along the street. "Do you think my car is here somewhere?"

"You drive a three-year-old red Mustang convertible." He didn't see the car, and that was strange. Where would Mallory have left it? Near the spot where the ambulance picked her up?

"Maybe someone stole it." Mallory scowled.

Gage didn't answer. An old-model beige Cadillac moved slowly down the street. Odd, how it didn't accelerate. Especially with no stop sign in sight. The clouds shifted from the sun and something glinted brightly from the partially open window of the backseat.

Long and narrow, he belatedly recognized the barrel of a gun.

"Get down!" Gage grabbed Mallory and shoved her down behind the parked cars. He dropped on top of her, protecting her body with his. Within seconds a storm of bullets showered the area around them.

FOUR

Glass shattered. People screamed. Debris spewed beneath a thunderous barrage of bullets. Squashed between the hard concrete and Gage's equally unyielding body, she listened to the violent assault, feeling helpless. The episode ended as quickly as it had started. After the roar of an engine and squealing tires echoed off the buildings, a stunned silence cloaked them.

"Are you okay?" Gage ran his hands urgently over her arms. "Say something, Mallory! Were you hit?"

"No. I'm okay." Her voice was barely a whisper. Yes, her body was bruised, but she was unharmed, thanks to Gage's quick reflexes. His unselfishness humbled her. He'd protected her with his life. Had anyone ever done that for her before? She had no way of knowing, but she somehow doubted it. She tried to raise her head to thank him.

"Stay down," Gage barked. Clearly he wasn't

lulled into complacency because the hail of gun-fire had ceased.

While she deeply appreciated his willingness to sacrifice himself, she couldn't breathe. Mallory tried to edge out from beneath Gage's suffocating weight. He must have figured out what was wrong, because he suddenly shifted to the right. She gulped in a huge breath of air, fighting a wave of dizziness.

Half of his body still shielded hers. Even in the desperate seriousness of the moment, she couldn't ignore her hyperawareness to his presence. Being held protectively by Gage was exciting yet familiar. Mallory kept her head low as she turned to see him, his face mere inches from hers. His eyes weren't the color of cinnamon anymore, but an intense chestnut-brown. His smooth jaw was clenched with anger, but his gaze was alert. For a guy, his sooty eyelashes were ridiculously long. His mouth was so close.

She had the insane urge to kiss him.

Their gazes locked, held. Mallory sucked in a quick breath. This was it. His eyes held the same awareness she was certain was in hers. Her heart quickened. Warm breath fanned her face. She stretched toward him—then froze when the distinct wail of police sirens filled the air.

Run! Run! Jerking her head toward the ominous sound, she sought a place to hide. Beneath one of the cars parked on the street? No. Too much glass carpeted the area between them. Around the building? Yes. There was time. They could make it. Wriggling against the weight of Gage's muscular limbs, she struggled to get free. He tightened his hold. She jammed her elbow in his ribs.

He grunted, his breath whooshing past her ear. "What's wrong with you? What are you doing?"

"Hurry!" she insisted. "We need to get out of here."

"Are you nuts? We can't leave. We're staying right here until the police arrive."

Before she could explain her unknown fears there were at least six or seven cops, covered from head to toe in full protective gear, surrounding them. Bile rose in her throat and she shrank against Gage's warmth, only this time he was the one who jerked away from the other's touch. The cops must have noticed their lack of weapons since they immediately fanned out, securing the area.

A tall officer with dark hair stayed behind. "I'm Officer Lowell. Are you okay? Anyone hurt?"

"We're fine." Gage swiftly rose to his feet. He hesitated for the barest fraction of a second before offering a hand to help her stand. "It's only a scratch."

A scratch? He was bleeding. Concern for Gage

pushed past her irrational fear. She hastily stood, her gaze focusing on the ominous bloodstain oozing through his white shirt. "Why didn't you tell me you were hurt?"

"I'm fine." He avoided eye contact, rejecting her concern.

Mallory ignored him and took his arm. A thin rivulet of blood dripped from his elbow. The image of a blood-stained wall flashed in her mind, but she swallowed hard and shook off the faint memory. "This isn't fine. It's a bullet wound." She pushed the sleeve of his shirt out of the way to better see the injury.

"I have a first-aid kit." Another officer stepped forward carrying a square box. "And there's an ambulance on the way."

Mallory plucked white squares of gauze from the first-aid kid. Gage's muscular arm was tense beneath her fingertips. His skin radiated heat. "Thankfully the bullet only grazed you. God was definitely watching over us."

"God?" Gage echoed in surprise.

"Don't you believe in God?" she asked. He stared at her for a long moment before he gave a curt nod. Satisfied, she turned back to his wound, covering the bloody gash with gauze and then glancing up at the officer with the first-aid kit. "Do you have an elastic bandage?"

"Sure." The cop handed her the roll.

"Thanks." She wrapped the elastic bandage around Gage's arm, anchoring the gauze in place. "This will work until the ambulance gets here. You should go to the hospital, although I don't think the wound will need stitches."

Gage frowned at her. "How would you know?"

Mallory was taken aback at his tone. How did she know? A memory? No, the black mist still dipped and swirled. Then she frowned. Basic common sense, that's how. "The gash isn't deep."

With a scowl he pulled away. "I'm fine, no reason to go to the hospital." Turning away, he gave his attention to the police officers.

His dismissal hurt. Far more than it should have. Tears threatened, but she refused to succumb, blaming them on delayed shock. What was wrong with her? Gage was off-limits. He cared about her sister. Had she imagined that moment when it seemed he might kiss her? Probably.

She'd been stressed, traumatized by the gunfire, and had imagined the brief, emotional connection. And really, why did she care? She barely knew her own name, much less anything about Gage. He might have strong shoulders that came in handy when he was protecting her, but he belonged to Alyssa. Right now she needed to concentrate on getting her memory back.

Every muscle in her body tensed when she noticed a tall, burly police officer climb from his squad car. Unlike the others, he was dressed in uniform minus the protective gear, as if he'd heard about the situation on the radio and had come to investigate. In the middle of the sidewalk, he halted midstride and stared at her.

Mallory's stomach dropped to her knees. She sucked in a raw breath. In a flash she remembered the same ruddy-faced officer glaring at her impatiently. Then the brief memory vanished like a puff of smoke. The fog rolled in. She wanted to scream in frustration.

A long billy club swayed from his waist as he approached. On the other hip, he wore a gun. His hand hovered near the weapon, his fingers caressing the metal as if he were a gunslinger ready to draw. Forcing herself to breathe, she eased closer to Gage. Deep in conversation with Officer Lowell, Gage didn't notice how the ruddy-faced cop trained his gaze on her as he approached. When he stopped in front of her, fear coated her mouth like dust.

"What's your name?" he demanded.

She tried to swallow but couldn't. She wanted to run. To hide. But she was safe next to Gage, right? A spurt of anger at his blatant attempt to intimidate her caused her to jut her chin. "Mallory Roth. Why? What's yours?"

The grooves in his flushed face deepened. "Officer Aaron Crane. Do you have ID?"

Mallory nodded, tempted to ask for his as she reached for her purse. She found her driver's license and handed it to him.

Gage finished his conversation, and she grasped his arm to get his attention. He subtly pulled away, putting a good foot of distance between them, but he turned to face Crane. "Is there a problem, officer?"

"No. No problem." Crane stared at her license for a long moment before handing it back to her. He glanced at Gage. "I'll need to see your identification, as well."

Gage jerked a thumb over his shoulder. "These guys have the information. I already gave them my statement."

"Oh, okay. Good." Officer Crane nodded abruptly then turned and walked away. Mallory heard him ask his fellow officers, "What happened here?"

Ignoring Gage's questioning look, she eavesdropped on the exchange between the cops, unable to strip her gaze from the stocky policeman. She didn't like him. More than that, she feared him. Why? Although irrational, she feared Officer Crane would arrest her if given the chance.

The cops' discussion turned toward gang violence. One witness reported seeing a flash of green from the Caddy's window, a color known to be favored by the Skidds gang. Their conclusion sounded logical, but she couldn't shake her reaction to Officer Crane. After a long hour, they were allowed to leave. Amazingly, Gage's truck parked a few cars down the street hadn't been damaged in the shootout. She caught a glimpse of Officer Crane staring after them as they drove off.

Her hands began to shake. She clasped them together in an effort to make them stop. Silently, she swiveled in her seat to stare at the receding figure of Officer Crane.

"Are you sure you're okay?" Gage's concern was a life preserver she grabbed with both hands. Just knowing she wasn't alone was a huge relief. She forced a smile.

"I'm not the one who was shot," she pointed out, striving for a light tone. She settled in her seat, hanging on to the sense of normalcy. She desperately needed to keep her mind off creepy Officer Crane.

"I wasn't shot. I was nicked." Gage shook his head. "Never mind. We need to make a quick stop before we check out those addresses."

For a moment she was confused. What addresses? Then she remembered. Alyssa's friends. Of course. They were on a mission to find Alyssa.

"Where?" She didn't really care where they went, as long as it was far away from the scene outside her apartment.

"My place. I have a few calls to make. I also need the charger for my cell phone."

"What kind of calls?"

Gage shrugged but didn't answer. She tried to think of something to talk about. Anything to keep from focusing on the horror of someone trying to kill them. Was this related to Alyssa? Had someone mistaken her for Alyssa? By the time Gage pulled in front of a quaint two-story white house, her body was shaking in earnest. She locked her hands beneath opposite elbows to maintain the illusion of control and followed Gage inside.

An overwhelming sense of coming home fused her feet to the floor. Gage ignored her as he headed for the phone. Half-dazed, Mallory stood in the center of the kitchen. Cheerful green-and-white-checkered curtains fluttered over the windows. With an effort, she forced herself to walk through the kitchen, down the hallway and into the bathroom.

Closing the door behind her, she sank onto the commode and buried her face in her hands.

She'd lost her mind. That was the only explanation. It was impossible to feel more comfortable at Gage's house than her own condo. She couldn't have spent much time here. She lived in the fancy downtown condo. *He loved Alyssa.*

She had to stop thinking about Gage. There were bigger problems to consider. Such as who was the older man in the picture? Why did the sight of Officer Crane fill her with such fear and dread? Did she really remember him? Or was it only someone who looked similar to him? The danger had passed. She and Gage were safe now.

Weren't they?

Maybe. If the shooting really was gang related. Had they really been in the wrong place at the wrong time? And if so, why had Officer Crane looked at her so strangely?

The Jefferson project. Mallory shivered. Maybe Alyssa was right. Maybe everything really was related to the Jefferson project.

Dear Lord, help me. Keep us safe. Mallory took several slow, deep breaths. *In, count to ten, then out and count to ten. Now start over again. Breathe in...*

Wait a minute. Where had she learned that? The dark haze still hovered in her mind, but she could sense she was getting close to remembering. As she'd remembered Crane. He wasn't just some look-alike. Closing her eyes, she could clearly bring the memory back. His irritated features as he glared down at her. *She remembered him.*

"Mallory?" Gage tapped on the door. "Are you okay?"

The hovering image vanished. "I'll be out in a minute." She rubbed her aching temples and splashed water on her face, staring at her reflection in the mirror.

She needed to be strong. Between them, she and Gage would figure out what was going on. This was not the time to fall apart. Or become preoccupied with her sister's boyfriend. Alyssa was in danger, either from the Jefferson project or the gang members themselves. Amnesia or not, Alyssa was counting on her.

And she was determined to be the kind of sister her twin deserved.

"Dan, I need your help." Gage held the phone propped between his chin and his shoulder. His stomach rumbled so loudly, he suspected his chief project manager could hear it. "What do you know about Hugh Jefferson?"

"Aside from the fact we're building his condos? Not much," Dan admitted. "He's a businessman from Chicago, dabbles in various investments but prefers real estate. He's a mover and a shaker. Likes the finer things in life."

"Yeah, but why is he suddenly buying property in Milwaukee? There must be dozens of places to expand in Chicago. Why is he coming up here?"

"I don't know. Why? Is there a problem?"

Gage didn't want to go into too much detail over the phone. "I have some serious reservations about the project, that's all."

"Do you want me to see if I can find out more about him?" Dan asked.

"Yeah, that would be good." The police wanted them to believe the attack outside Mallory's apartment building was random. Gang activity was heating up, they'd claimed. The chief of police and the mayor had teamed up to form a special task force aimed at bringing gang activity under control. Today's shooting was a perfect example of why the task force was so important.

But Gage didn't buy it. He couldn't ignore the string of coincidences. First Ray Schaefer died of stab wounds. Now this attack outside Mallory's apartment. Alyssa seemingly missing.

He should have listened to Alyssa from the start, the night she'd called him from the E.D. He'd failed her. Again. The first time when he'd let her walk away, and the second when he hadn't believed her. Pushing back a wave of helpless regret, he struggled to think. Okay, say the Jefferson project was dangerous. Why? Who was involved? At what level?

"…meet me later?"

Gage belatedly realized Dan was waiting for a response. "Huh? Yeah, I know it's Saturday, but let's meet later. In the downtown office at six."

"Okay. I did find out something strange the other day, but let me look into things a bit and I'll fill you in later."

He was tempted to push Dan for more information, but just then Mallory entered the kitchen. "Fine. I'll see you later, Dan." Gage hung up the phone and slowly turned to face her.

"I remembered something."

Pale yet determined, Mallory stood in the center of his kitchen. Alyssa's kitchen. The one she'd taken such pleasure in helping him decorate. The green-and-white curtains had been her choice.

"Didn't you hear me?" she said again, impatiently. "I remembered something."

He blinked and straightened. "What did you remember?"

"The cop."

"Which cop?" As soon as he asked, he knew. The guy who'd approached and asked for her ID. He'd thought her reaction was strange at the time. Her fear of the officer had been palpable.

"Officer Aaron Crane."

"What about him? What exactly did you remember?" Gage held his breath, hoping and praying she would remember.

"Just his face, really. But I know I've seen him someplace before. I tapped his arm to get his attention and he glanced down at me with angry annoyance. That's all I remember."

She was right, it wasn't much. "Anything else? Where were you? Why were you talking to a cop? Were you with your twin? Maybe filling out a police report or something like that?"

Her brows pulled together in a deep frown. She rubbed the ache in her left temple then slowly shook her head. "I don't know. I'm sorry, I can't remember."

Her apology sounded so much like Alyssa. The way she'd mentioned how God had watched over them was also something Alyssa would say.

Not Mallory.

Alyssa had vowed not to take Mallory's identity ever again, but what if she thought her life was in danger? Would that be enough to cause her to forsake her vow?

Yes. Slowly realization dawned. Of course it would. "You're Alyssa."

"What?" She stared at him as if he were crazy. "My ID says otherwise."

He couldn't believe he hadn't figured it out sooner. The way she'd known the woman in the hospital waiting room was going to respiratory arrest—just the first of many clues. And he'd ignored them all. "You're not Mallory, you're Alyssa." He knew he was right. An overwhelming relief washed over him. He wanted to hold her.

"And you know this—how?"

The anger in her voice jerked him back to reality. "It's the only thing that makes sense. Earlier you asked me if I believed in God, and I do. So does Alyssa. But Mallory is not a churchgoer. Aly...*you* talked about it."

Slowly she shook her head. "I think you're just saying this to make yourself feel better."

"Feel better about what?" he demanded.

"About how close we came to kissing back there on the sidewalk."

He remembered that moment, when their faces had been close. Too close. "Nothing happened," he denied swiftly. "What's wrong with you? I thought you'd be glad to know your true identity."

"But I don't know my true identity, do I?" she countered. "Telling me I'm Alyssa or Mallory doesn't really change anything. I'm not anyone until I can remember for myself."

He didn't want to admit she was right. He knew she had to be Alyssa. Even from here he could see how her rose and dagger tattoo had faded. But while he might be convinced she really was Alyssa, the truth didn't change anything.

She still couldn't remember. Not her identity and not anything related to the danger they were in.

Danger. The realization hit him like a ton of bricks. If the Jefferson project was at the root of the danger, they couldn't stay in his house. Wouldn't that be the first place they'd look? He and Alyssa needed to get out of here, before his suburban neighborhood became the site of another supposed gang shoot-out.

"We can't stay here," he said, abruptly changing the subject. "We'll grab something to eat and then pack a couple of bags."

"Leave?" she frowned. "But we just got here."

"I know." He wished they could stay, because it was possible that being in familiar surroundings would help her memory to return. "We'll have to find a safe place to hide until we find out what's going on."

She didn't look convinced. "You really think we're in danger?"

"Yes, I do. But, Alyssa, you don't have to be afraid. I promise I'll protect you."

She scowled. "Don't call me Alyssa."

He was taken aback by her curt tone. "I have to

call you something," he said, trying to sound reasonable. "Trust me, I know you're Alyssa."

"I do trust you to protect me," she said, her expression bleak. "But I can't be Alyssa or Mallory. I can't be anyone, not until my memory returns."

FIVE

Hugging herself, she turned her back on Gage, not wanting him to realize how close she was to completely breaking down. Why was he pursuing this? As much as Mallory's fancy condo didn't seem right, she couldn't simply accept his theory that she was really Alyssa.

This had to be some sort of defense mechanism on his part. A way for Gage to ease his guilt. He could deny it until the cows came home, but she knew they'd been close to kissing once they'd realized they were safe on the sidewalk. It hadn't been just her imagination. Obviously, he needed a way to excuse his behavior, by convincing himself she was Alyssa and not Mallory.

"Aly—look, I'm sorry. I know this is a lot for you to take in at one time. And I wish we could stay here until you do. We need to leave as soon as possible. Would you mind making sandwiches while I throw some things into a couple of duffel bags?"

Letting out her breath in a sigh, she reluctantly nodded. "Sure. I should be able to manage that."

"Thank you," he murmured softly, his gaze compassionate. His gratitude was almost too much to bear. It was easier when he acted as if he didn't like her. She'd convinced herself she had to keep her distance from him because he belonged to Alyssa.

But what if he really belonged to her? The mere thought made her heart race.

Now which one of them was taking the easy way out? Annoyed with herself, she waited until Gage left the kitchen before turning her attention to the task at hand. Now that he'd mentioned food, she realized she was terribly hungry. Sandwiches sounded good, so she crossed over to the bread box and found a loaf of light wheat bread, exactly the kind she liked. She found a butter knife in the silverware drawer and was opening the fridge before she realized she'd known exactly where the silverware was kept.

Could he be right? Was she really Alyssa?

Or could it be that Mallory had spent some time here, too, and also would have known where the silverware was kept? Actually, the more she thought about it, the more she realized the drawer, wider than the others, was the most logical place to keep silverware. The way she'd gone there first had nothing to do with having a buried memory.

And obviously, psychoanalyzing herself to death wouldn't help. The doctor had said her memory would return, and she had little choice but to believe him. She'd remembered Crane, right? The rest would come in time.

She found fresh turkey, lettuce, tomato and mayo for their sandwiches and quickly made several, figuring Gage would need at least two to keep him satisfied.

The first cupboard she opened didn't contain the paper bags, but she found them eventually and packed the sandwiches along with crisp green apples for their lunch.

"Are you ready?" Gage asked when he returned.

"Yes." She frowned when she saw the two duffel bags he had slung over his shoulder. "You have clothes for me in there, too?" she asked with dismay. She couldn't explain why the idea bothered her so much.

He flushed and shook his head. "No. But I have some sweatpants, T-shirts and sweatshirts for you to wear. We can't go back to Mallory's condo, it's not safe. Although, I suppose if you really want to wear your own clothes, we could stop at Alyssa's town house to pick up a few things."

A few hours ago, she would have jumped on the chance to get some different clothes, something comfortable to wear. Now, she sensed this was just another way for Gage to prove she was Alyssa. She shook her head, wincing at the flash of pain. Her headache still lingered in the recesses of her brain, no matter how much she tried to ignore it. "No, that's all right. Sweatpants and sweatshirts are fine with me. I'm always cold anyway."

"If you're sure," Gage said slowly. The way he looked at her with such an intent gaze made her uncomfortable. She could tell he was trying to figure out what was going on in her mind, especially since she didn't want to be called Alyssa. How could she explain what she didn't understand herself? "Let me know if you change your mind," he added. "If you're ready, let's get going. We can eat in the car on the way to visit Emma Banks and Paige Sanders."

"We're still going to question them, even though you think I'm Alyssa?" she challenged.

He looked surprised at her question. "You said yourself, you don't remember anything. And I guess I don't have proof, except for your faith. But it doesn't matter, really, because at this point, I need all the information they can give me."

She couldn't argue his logic, so she followed him outside, carrying the lunch bags. He'd changed into a short-sleeved knit shirt, and the muscles in his arms flexed as he tucked the bags safely behind the front seat of the truck. The elastic wrap was still covering the wound in his upper arm, and she made a mental note to change the dressing again later, to make sure the injury didn't get infected.

When the bullets had peppered the air around them, he'd covered her body with his, protecting her from harm. He'd never so much as muttered a complaint when he'd been hit. She was awed by his strength and protectiveness.

And she couldn't deny she was attracted to him. Still, she was determined not to act on her feelings until she'd regained her memories of him. Of their relationship. If there was a relationship to remember.

She climbed into the passenger seat beside him, fearing that telling herself to ignore the tumultuous feelings she had for Gage would prove far easier than actually doing it.

She watched warily as Gage's expression grew dark and grim as the day progressed. Checking with Paige and Emma proved futile. Both nurses denied seeing Alyssa other than the last time they'd worked together. Paige had been shocked at the news about Alyssa's leave of absence, and she couldn't offer any ideas about where Alyssa might have gone or whether or not she believed she was in danger.

Emma, on the other hand, had stared at her in

shock when they met her at the door. To avoid confusion, she'd introduced herself as Mallory. After all, that was the name on her driver's license. "I thought you were sick," Emma said.

"What do you mean?" she asked with a frown.

"Alyssa told me she needed some time off because of her sister." Emma shrugged. "I guess I assumed you were sick."

"No. I'm not sick." She exchanged a long glance with Gage. Apparently Alyssa's time off work had been carefully planned. Had Mallory helped Alyssa with her plan? She wished she knew. "Did Alyssa say anything else?"

Emma shook her head. "'Fraid not."

She nodded and smiled. "Thanks for your help."

Gage fished a business card from his pocket and handed it to Emma. He'd given one to Paige, too. "If you hear from Alyssa, will you please call me? Doesn't matter if it's day or night, just call."

If he was putting on an act for Emma's benefit, he deserved to win an award. The anguish in his tone made clear his feelings for Alyssa. For her? Her heart surged with hope and she ruthlessly squashed it. She turned away, determined to keep her distance.

Neither of them spoke as they walked back to his truck. She forced herself to think about what they'd learned. Alyssa must have planned to disappear, which only lent credence to Gage's theory.

"You realize that if I'm Alyssa, Mallory is the one who's missing," she said after several long moments.

He shot her a quick glance. "Yeah, that thought occurred to me, too."

"So maybe we're going about this all wrong," she mused. "Maybe we need to be searching for Mallory. Rick Weber is her boss. Maybe he knows something."

Gage shrugged. "Seems to me Rick couldn't know much, since he left a message for Mallory about the Jefferson project. Besides, I don't get the impression Mallory is particularly close to her boss."

"Who is she close to?"

"You."

Her breath caught in her throat. "You mean—she's close to Alyssa."

He didn't answer for a minute, his attention on the road. Emma Banks lived outside the city, and the traffic on the freeway was particularly heavy, thanks to summer construction. He slowed to a crawl. "We're supposed to meet my project manager, Dan Kirkland, downtown in thirty minutes. At this rate, we're going to be late."

She let him change the subject, because really,

why belabor the point? Deep down, she knew she'd rather be Alyssa than Mallory. Mallory lived a lifestyle she wasn't sure she liked. The condo was fancy, but not to her taste. But she also couldn't deny that there could be a very good reason for Mallory to hide her true nature beneath a facade. Maybe the older guy in the glossy photo had done something to hurt Mallory. Maybe that's why Mallory had looked sad standing next to a glowing Alyssa.

If she was really Mallory, then she'd accept herself for who she was. If she'd made mistakes in the past, then fine. She'd deal with that and move on.

God forgave all sins. Surely he'd forgive Mallory's sins. Whatever they were.

"I'm getting off the freeway," Gage muttered. "This traffic is ridiculous."

Her ankle throbbed and she opened her purse to find her pills, only to realize she left them on the kitchen counter. "Gage, do you think it's safe to go back to the condo for a few minutes?"

"What?" He looked over at her. "Why?"

"I forgot my pain medication," she admitted, worrying her lower lip with her teeth. "But if you think it's too dangerous, then I'll live without them."

Gage let out a sigh. "No one would expect us to

go back, so it's probably fine. As long as we don't stay too long."

"Just enough to get my pills," she promised.

Gage drove past the high-rise condo once, looking over the area. The mess was mostly cleaned up and the police had left the area. He circled the block before pulling into an empty parking space a few blocks from the doorway. Even then, he hesitated for a long moment until he finally turned toward her.

"Will you wait here for me?" he asked. "No need for both of us to go in."

She shook her head. "Don't leave me outside alone, please, Gage. What if the gunman comes back? I'd rather be with you."

He hesitated and then nodded. "Okay, we need to be in and out in less than five minutes." His serious gaze met hers. "Ready?"

She pulled out her keys and then clutched her purse tightly. "Yes. I'm ready."

Gage took the keys and, moving swiftly, they both climbed out of his truck and headed into the building. The glass elevator was waiting for them on the ground floor and they hurried to step inside. The ride to the top floor took forever, and she couldn't help feeling completely exposed the way they were practically surrounded with glass. Once outside her door, Gage took her arm and moved her protectively behind him. He used her key to open the door and kicked it with his foot before daring to poke his head inside.

The red, blue and black condo appeared empty. The only real place to hide was in her bedroom. He led the way down the hall, making sure the room was clear before stepping back to allow her to enter the kitchen. The small pill bottle wasn't on the counter. In the bathroom? She hurried down the hall and into the bathroom, picking up the medication she'd left there.

Since she was right near the bedroom, she took a few minutes to stuff some underwear into her purse, too. She returned to the living room in less than two minutes. "I'm ready."

"Good. Let's go."

They rode the elevator down to the lobby. On the way out, she noticed, through the wide-envelope slot, that her mailbox was full. Glancing at her keys, she made a quick detour.

"What are you doing?" he asked.

"The mailbox is full, probably from yesterday's delivery. Don't you think it would be best to empty it out?"

"Good thinking." His approval made her smile. She simply shoved the mail into her purse, which was bulging by this point. They easily made it back out to Gage's truck well within their allotted time frame. He kept a hand under her elbow, herding her toward their vehicle. He gave her a boost up into the truck before skirting around to climb in beside her. Gage pulled away, and she sat back in relief as they left the fancy condo building behind.

"Your purse looks like it's going to explode," Gage teased.

She blushed, refusing to tell him she'd stuffed underwear in there, too. Sweatpants and T-shirts were fine, but she needed underclothes, as well. "Where are we going to spend the night?"

"Good question." He kept his gaze on the road as he navigated several turns. "I'd like to talk to Dan first, and then figure out where to go from there."

She knew Gage was hoping Dan would have information for them. But what if he didn't? They needed answers, and her lack of memory certainly wasn't helping their situation.

She closed her eyes and focused on the brief recognition of Officer Crane. For a nanosecond, she could clearly see the taut lines of irritation on his ruddy face. When had she spoken to him? Where were they? At the police station perhaps? She had the impression of sterile-looking walls behind him. The feeling of doom persisted. And she couldn't help but wonder—would the return of her memory bring concrete reasons for the elusive sense of danger?

* * *

Gage tried to keep his eyes on the road, but he couldn't help sending quick sidelong glances over to Alyssa. He couldn't understand her reluctance to be called Alyssa, especially when he knew, deep down, that's who she really was.

It was the only thing that made sense.

Retrograde amnesia, the doctor had said. A temporary loss of memory around a specific, traumatic event. But amnesia wouldn't change someone's personality. And the woman sitting beside him acted and sounded like Alyssa.

But if she was Alyssa, then maybe they really should be searching for Mallory. Their parents had died a few years ago, leaving a modest inheritance for the twins. He knew Alyssa had put her half of the money into a savings account, planning to use some for their wedding.

But if Mallory needed it, she'd give it to her sister without so much as a second thought. With cash, Mallory could be anywhere.

Gage pulled into the parking garage across the street from the high-rise building that housed Drummond Builders Inc. The parking attendant on duty greeted him cheerfully when he rolled down the window. "Good evening, Mr. Drummond."

"Good evening to you, too, Curtis." Gage pulled through the gate and parked in the first available space. After shutting off his truck, he got out and went around to open the passenger door for Alyssa. He knew she had a sore ankle, so he didn't say anything about how they were running late for their six o'clock meeting with Dan.

Alyssa's gaze swept the area, as if she'd never seen this part of the city before. Which he knew wasn't true, since she'd come to visit him here often. "Anything look familiar?" he asked casually.

"No, sorry." They walked together across the street and into the building. Alyssa continued to glance around as if seeing everything for the first time. Inside the chrome-and-glass office building, she waited for him to lead the way.

He tried not to show his disappointment. He'd really hoped Alyssa might remember his office building. They entered a quiet, conventional elevator and he pushed the button for the tenth floor.

"Only the tenth floor?" She cocked an eyebrow at him. "Not the penthouse suite? I'm shocked."

Her teasing made him smile. He and Alyssa had bantered like this a lot, before she'd broken off their engagement. "I'm lucky to afford downtown rent at all," he murmured. "The penthouse is out of my league."

"Can you afford to stay here, even without the Jefferson project?" she asked.

Slowly, he shook his head. "Probably not." He'd

worked hard to grow the business over these past few years. His father had retired three years ago, yet their reputation for doing great work lived on. Branching out with something as big as the Jefferson project had been a risk, but one that had paid off. Or so he thought. Now, pulling out of the project would damage his reputation, and without other projects, he'd very likely have to downsize.

The idea that he might lose his business altogether made him feel sick. The subtle ding of the elevator brought him out of his grim thoughts. The doors silently slid open. The main office was closed for the weekend. Gage and his chief project manager were probably the only two who could be found working at odd hours, day or night, doing whatever it took to get the job done on time and under budget.

He unlocked the office door and stepped over the threshold. The summer sky poured in through the windows. Still, he flicked on the overhead lights so Dan would know they were here. He crossed the room, his footsteps muffled on the thick carpet.

"Nice place," Alyssa commented.

He nodded an acknowledgment but didn't answer. The message light on the office phone wasn't lit. He pulled out his cell phone, checking to see if he'd missed a message from Dan letting him know he'd be late.

No message, so he called Dan himself. But the call went directly to Dan's voice mail. Why wouldn't Dan have his phone on? Gage closed his phone with a snap. Where was he? Dan was rarely late.

"Problems?" Alyssa asked, sensing his mood.

"No. Dan will be here soon." He decided not to voice his concern. Alyssa had enough to worry about.

She arched her brow as if she didn't believe him, a gesture that keenly reminded him of Alyssa. "So, how about giving me the grand tour while we wait?" she suggested.

Gage couldn't think of a reason not to. Showing her around might spark her memory. And besides, anything was better than standing around staring at each other. He waved a hand at the office around him. "This is the main office. My assistant, Jane Hanson, sits here and generally manages to keep everything running smoothly."

He turned and walked toward the back of the room, where several other doors were located. "My office is through here." He unlocked the door farthest to the right and opened it. As owner of the business, he'd earned the corner office, complete with ceiling-to-floor windows. He didn't mention the attacks of vertigo that hit him when he stood too close to them. After flicking on the lights, he stepped back to allow Alyssa to enter.

She walked past him, brushing ever so slightly against him. She whistled softly under her breath when she saw the plush office complete with beautiful mahogany furniture. She headed straight for the windows. "Can you see Lake Michigan from here?"

"Uh—yeah. Sort of." He ventured farther into the room but didn't join her by the windows. He didn't like to stand so close, looking down. "To the right of the Art Museum you can make out the gleam of the lake."

"Oh, I see it now." She flashed him a warm smile over her shoulder. "Very nice. I really hope you don't have to give this up." Her eyes filled with concern.

"Me, either." It wouldn't be the first time he'd have to start from scratch. After his mother died, he and his father had lived hand-to-mouth, moving from one construction job to the next. Once he'd finished high school, their business had taken off to the point where they were financially secure. He'd thought it was a perfect time to get married, start a family.

Then things had fallen apart with Alyssa. And now the Jefferson project was surrounded in danger. Squashing the flash of helplessness, he stepped back so Alyssa could come back out. He closed and locked the door behind her.

"Whose offices are these?" She gestured to the remaining two doors.

"One is Dan's office. The other is actually a conference room. We run a pretty lean staff. I have several assistant project managers, but they stay on the job sites rather than camp out here. The most important part of our work isn't done within these walls."

"I can understand that. So the Jefferson project isn't the only one you're working on?" Alyssa reached out to try Dan's office door. The handle turned smoothly beneath the pressure of her hand and the door swung open.

"It's not locked," she said, stating the obvious.

Gage frowned and squeezed past her to enter the office, flipping on a light switch as he went. He could feel Alyssa following close behind him. Barely two steps into the room, he nearly tripped over the body lying on the floor.

Beside him, Alyssa cried out in horror. Grimly, he stared at the vacant, lifeless gaze of his chief project manager and the knife buried deep in his chest. Gage bit back a wave of impotent grief.

Dan hadn't been late for their meeting after all.

SIX

She stumbled backward, away from the dark stain on Dan Kirkland's chest. Blood. There was so much blood. She tried to close her eyes but the blood was everywhere, smeared on the walls and pooled on the floor. And in the far corner of the room, a bloody yellow blouse. She sobbed, overwhelmed with grief. *Mallory!*

"Alyssa!"

She blinked and the image faded. She was surprised to realize she was sitting on the floor, her back against the office wall and Gage looming over her. He had a worried expression as he knelt at her side. "Are you okay?"

She swallowed a wave of nausea and nodded. The image had been so real, but what did it mean? Where had she seen so much blood? She wanted to believe the bloody room was too horrible to be real, except for the bloodstains on her jeans. She gulped a huge breath of air and tried to swallow her panic. Dazed, she glanced around. How on earth had she gotten out of Dan's office, to the farthest side of the room, closest to the door?

"You shouted your sister's name." His gaze was full of compassionate concern. "Did you remember something? Something about your twin?"

The foggy haze was back and her temple ached. She was oddly reluctant to tell Gage about the blood and the yellow blouse. Was it really a memory? The sense of danger returned more forceful than ever. "I shouted Mallory's name?"

"Yes, when you saw Dan, and then you ran away." Gage sat back on his heels, scrubbing a hand over his face. "I don't blame you for being upset. I can't believe he's dead."

A real dead body was far worse than a bloody room. "How?" she whispered.

"A knife wound to the chest. His wallet is lying on the floor next to him, empty. Cash and credit cards are missing."

Alyssa started to tremble. "Robbery? You're saying this is a result of a simple mugging?"

"That's what they want us to believe, but there's no way this is anything simple." His hands shook, ever so slightly, and he closed them into fists. "We need to call the police."

"No!" her response was immediate. Intense. She grabbed his arm, hanging on tight. "Don't."

For a long minute Gage stared at her. Then he slowly stood, gently pulling her up onto her feet. "Alyssa, I have to. He was more than an employee, he was my friend. I can't leave him lying there. He has family, an ex-wife, parents. We have to call somebody. Especially when you and I know very well this isn't a random mugging."

Alyssa put a hand to her throat, the pressure in her chest so tight she could hardly breathe. "Let's get out of here first, and then call someone to investigate."

He frowned. "The police will want to talk to us, since we found the body."

She couldn't explain the deep fear twisting around inside. "Please, Gage? We can't stay here. We have to leave. Now." *Run! Run! Get as far from the blood and police as possible. Run!* She grabbed Gage's arm and tugged him toward the door. She'd drag him the whole way if necessary.

"Okay, okay, let me think." He hung back, halting her progress, and reached for his phone. "I left a message with Jonah earlier today. Jonah Stewart is a detective with the Milwaukee Police Department. He and I have been friends since high school. I'd trust him with my life. I'll call him for help."

The thought of going to the police terrified her, but surely they could trust Gage's high school friend. "We can call him once we're safely away from here. Please?" She couldn't explain the desperate need to escape. What if Crane was on his way here already? The guy had a knack for showing up at crime scenes.

The stark fear in her gaze must have gotten to him, because he finally relented. "Okay, let's go. I'll try him later."

She couldn't get out of the office suite fast enough. Gage walked over to the elevators and pushed the down button. Both cars were on the ground floor. "Let's take the stairs."

"Ten flights? Are you crazy?" he asked.

"Down is easy. Come on." She refused to take no for an answer. She headed into the stairwell, instinctively knowing Gage wouldn't let her go alone. She took the stairs down as quickly as she could manage on her ankle. The sounds of pounding feet intermingled with their heavy breathing. Alyssa didn't stop until they reached the ground floor.

She opened the door on the ground level with trepidation. Thankfully, the lobby of the office building was deserted. When they walked past the elevators, she noticed they were both on the tenth floor. Would both elevators be summoned at the push of a button? Or had someone ridden to the tenth floor to find them? Someone like Officer Crane?

She couldn't explain her paranoia, so she kept

her wild thoughts to herself. Tugging on Gage's arm, she led the way outside and across the street to the parking garage where they'd left his truck. Dark apprehension clenched her belly and she couldn't relax, even when the parking lot attendant gave them a cheerful wave as they drove away.

Gage navigated the streets, his thoughts in turmoil. He still couldn't believe Dan Kirkland was dead. The image of Dan's vacant gaze and the bloody knife embedded deep in his chest haunted him. His grief was nearly overwhelming, but he held himself together with an effort, knowing Alyssa needed him to be strong. There would be time to mourn the passing of his friend later.

He darted a glance over to Alyssa. She was still pale, huddled in the seat as if chilled, although the temperature outside was warm. Her blue eyes were unnaturally bright, indicating she was still in shock.

She'd screamed when they'd all but stumbled across Dan's inert body and then had backed away, huddling against the opposite wall, sobbing and crying out her sister's name. He feared something terrible may have happened to Alyssa. Something traumatic that ultimately caused her amnesia.

And why was she so afraid of the police? Not just the officer she'd remembered at the scene outside Mallory's condo, but apparently all police. Why would she be so frightened? What secret was hidden in her locked memory? He risked another sidelong glance, thankful to note her cheeks had regained a bit of color.

Hearing her call out Mallory's name had cemented his belief that she was Alyssa.

"Where are we going?" she asked in a low tone, as if feeling his gaze upon her.

"A small motel outside of town. A place called the Forty Winks motel. They'll take cash with no questions asked." Gage rubbed a hand over his eyes, fighting exhaustion. Although Alyssa looked far worse than he felt.

He wanted to hold her close, to offer comfort. But he forced himself to keep his distance. She didn't remember him, and for the first time, it occurred to him that when she did remember, she'd know exactly why she'd left him.

Gage forced himself to concentrate on their next steps. Once they arrived at the motel, he'd need to get in touch with Jonah to help take care of Dan. He couldn't help feeling guilty that they hadn't gotten to the office sooner. Maybe if they hadn't been late, Dan would still be alive. Had his project manager discovered something incriminating related to the Jefferson project? Was that why someone stabbed him? There were several homicides in Milwaukee every month. But there were now at least two deaths connected to the Jefferson project, and that wasn't a coincidence.

Gage gripped the steering wheel so tightly his knuckles turned white. There was a part of him that wanted to go back to the office building to go through whatever paperwork Dan might have reviewed. But Alyssa had been so upset, he hadn't had the heart to refuse her request. He had no choice but to believe the gunfire outside Mallory's condo had been a warning to stay away, or worse, an attempt to kill them. Either way, he couldn't take a chance with her life.

He'd do anything to keep her safe. And for the first time in months, he silently prayed.

Dear Lord, please give me the knowledge and strength to keep Alyssa safe.

The rooms in the Forty Winks motel were worse than he remembered. Thankfully, they had two adjoining rooms. The two-story building had thirty rooms, all facing outside. He'd requested rooms on the first floor farthest from the office.

He unlocked the first door and crossed over to set the duffel he'd packed for Alyssa on the bed. He unlocked the connecting door between their rooms and then retraced his steps to the main door.

"Alyssa, you need to keep that connecting door open, okay?"

She stood uncertainly in the center of the room, looking fragile, as if a strong wind would blow her away. "Sure."

Once again, he longed to take her into his arms to offer comfort. Instead, he walked back outside and entered the second motel room. He opened his connecting door and noticed Alyssa had disappeared into the bathroom.

His phone rang, and he was pleased to see the caller was Jonah. "I'm so glad you called me back," he said gratefully.

"You sounded desperate. What's up?"

"I have a big problem, Jonah. I really need your help."

"Lucky for you, I just finished up a case, so I have some vacation time coming," Jonah said, his voice sharp with interest.

Gage hesitated. He'd known Jonah long before he'd become a homicide detective, but this wasn't the sort of bomb you dropped over the phone. "If you don't mind, I'd rather talk to you in person."

"No problem," Jonah agreed readily enough. "Where are you? I can leave right now."

Relieved, Gage gave his friend directions to their motel. If Jonah thought the Forty Winks was a strange meeting place, he didn't let on. After promising to be there soon, he hung up.

Gage immediately felt better. Jonah was a good detective, and he'd know what to do. There wasn't much to unpack, so he paced the length of his room, staying away from the connecting door but listening to the muffled thumps as Alyssa moved around.

Soon, she came over to stand in the open doorway between their rooms. Her hair was damp, and she'd changed her clothes, the neckline of his oversize T-shirt giving a glimpse of the rose and dagger tattoo just beneath her collarbone. The tattoo was more faded than ever.

"Did you get hold of your cop friend?" she asked.

"Uh, yeah." He sighed and scrubbed a hand over his face. "Jonah has met Alyssa before, so I'll have to explain about your amnesia."

She grimaced but nodded. "I understand."

There was a sharp knock at his motel door. Gage jumped up and crossed over, peering through the peephole to verify that Jonah was the one standing on the other side. Darkness had fallen, but the evenly spaced lights between the rooms were bright enough for him to easily recognize his friend.

He unlocked the chain and opened the door.

"Jonah." He thumped his buddy on the back in greeting. "I can't tell you how glad I am to see you."

"Same here. I have to say, you piqued my curiosity." Jonah wore regular street clothes but the shoulder harness housing his gun was reassuring. "What's going on?"

Gage drew Jonah inside. "Jonah, you remember Alyssa, don't you?"

"Uh, yeah. Sure." Jonah studied her, looking uncomfortable. "Nice to see you again, Alyssa."

A faint smile touched her lips. "I'd say the same if I could remember you, Jonah," she murmured.

Jonah's jaw dropped in shock. "Alyssa hit her head and has amnesia," Gage hastily explained. He pulled up one of the two straight-back chairs. "Sit down, Jonah, and let me explain everything from the beginning."

Jonah sank into the seat, a dazed expression on his face. Alyssa sat on the bed, hugging her knees to her chest.

"I told you how I won the bid for the Jefferson project, right?" Gage asked. Jonah nodded. "Three days ago, City Councilman Ray Schaefer was brought into Trinity's E.D. after he was stabbed in the chest."

Jonah frowned. "Yeah, I heard he was the victim of a gang-initiation prank."

"Not true." Gage held Jonah's gaze with his. "Alyssa was working the trauma room that night. The councilman told her what really happened." Gage filled in the details.

Jonah's eyes widened, and he glanced over at Alyssa. "Did you talk to anyone else about this?"

"I don't know," Alyssa whispered. "I can't remember."

Jonah scowled, his expression clearly saying he didn't believe her. "You can't remember anything? Are you sure?"

"Knock it off, Jonah. Her amnesia is real and you need to let me finish. I didn't take Alyssa's concerns seriously, and I think she must be in danger." He hated himself for letting Alyssa down. "And to make matters worse, Mallory is missing."

"We should file a missing person's report, right away." Jonah leaned forward, in full cop mode.

"There's more," Gage cautioned. "Earlier today, when Alyssa and I were leaving Mallory's condo, someone opened fire on us, shooting from the back window of a rusty beige Cadillac. When the police arrived, they told us we were victims of gang violence."

"Yeah, there have been reports of increasing gang violence in the form of random shootings," Jonah admitted.

"Both Ray Schaefer and us?" Gage raised his

eyebrows in disbelief. "I don't think so, because the problems don't stop there. I called my chief project manager, Dan Kirkland. I told him I had serious reservations about the Jefferson project. I explained how Alyssa was convinced it was dangerous. He mentioned he'd found something odd, but he wanted to verify it first. We made arrangements to meet at six o'clock this evening. But we were late. We thought he wasn't there, but then we stumbled upon his dead body." His voice turned husky with grief. He cleared his throat and forced himself to continue. "Dan had been stabbed in the chest, his wallet lying empty beside him."

"Two people associated with the project dead and one attempt on your life." Jonah slowly summarized the key events, his expression grim. "I don't like it. I don't like it at all."

Relief washed over him. He and Alyssa weren't alone, not anymore. "Exactly my point. And Schaefer was stabbed, too, just like Dan."

"Okay, but why call me?" Jonah asked, perplexed. "Why not call the police?"

"Jonah, you're the only cop I know on a personal level, and to be honest we don't know who to trust. The Jefferson project was hotly contested and there's a lot of money on the line. For all we know, anyone could be involved in this."

Jonah raised his brow. "You mean like the mayor?"

"Possibly. Why not?" He shrugged. "Expensive, luxury condos mean a nice increase in city taxes. Eric Holden has only been the interim mayor for a few weeks, since Mayor Flynn's unexpected death from a massive heart attack. They're holding a special election on Tuesday to make things official, aren't they? The timing is suspicious. Could be someone who works for Holden. Or the city. There could be cops involved."

"Creepy Crane," Alyssa said suddenly.

"Who?" Jonah turned in his seat to face her.

"Aaron Crane. He's a cop."

Jonah frowned. "And you don't like him?"

Alyssa slowly shook her head. "I don't trust him. He was one of the cops who came to the scene outside the condo. The way he stared at me—I can't describe it."

"You're a beautiful woman, Alyssa." Jonah shrugged diplomatically. "Can't arrest a guy for being interested in a beautiful woman."

"No, it wasn't that." Alyssa waved a hand in annoyance. "He stared at me as if he'd seen a ghost. He wanted to know my name and asked to see my ID."

"We always check IDs at the scene of a crime," Jonah said in exasperation. "So what?"

"They checked mine, too, remember," Gage added, supporting his friend.

"It was almost as if he knew me," Alyssa persisted. "And now that I think about it, I gave him Mallory's ID. Maybe that's the only reason he let me go."

Gage was glad she'd seemed to accept she really was Alyssa, but now that she mentioned how Crane looked at her ID, he found he was glad she'd borrowed Mallory's identity. Especially if it kept her safe.

Jonah sighed heavily. "I have to admit, I never liked Crane. He's far too arrogant for his own good. But that doesn't mean he's involved in this. We need facts, not gut feelings." Jonah turned toward Gage. "I don't suppose you've notified the police about finding Dan Kirkland's body in your office?"

The expression on Gage's face must have told the whole story.

"Great, just great." Jonah pushed his fingers through his sun-streaked hair. "I have to call this in, and it's going to look suspicious that you came here first."

"Alyssa was upset, shaking. I had to get her out of there," Gage said slowly. "But you have to tell them she's Mallory and that we left because we didn't know if the killer was lurking around somewhere."

"Okay, that works," Jonah agreed. "As a homicide detective, I can investigate his death, but that means I need to get over there right away."

"Thanks, Jonah. I owe you one," Gage said gratefully.

"Yeah." Jonah stood. "But hey, what are friends for? Just don't go anywhere, because after I examine the crime scene I'll have to officially interview both of you. We need to follow the book as close as possible on this."

"We're not going anywhere." Gage kept his gaze from straying to where Alyssa still sat on the bed. Her hair had dried and now waved softly around her face.

"Okay, then. Give me a couple of hours to get everything I need from the crime scene." Jonah didn't appear to mind the prospect of a long night ahead of him. His eyes were bright with interest. Gage knew his buddy loved nothing more than solving a good puzzle.

"Like I said, we'll be here." Gage followed him to the door. When he left, Gage called out, "Jonah?" His friend glanced over his shoulder questioningly. "Be careful. If Dan's death is related to the Jefferson project, you could be in danger, too. Especially if the danger is from inside."

"Don't worry, I know how to handle this." Confident as ever, Jonah raised a hand as he left.

Gage watched him leave, the gnawing in his gut

worsening with every step. Jonah was a good cop. One of the best. He could take care of himself. Gage let out a heavy sigh and shut the door, flipping the dead bolt and then looping the chain lock for added security. Both locks were relatively useless against the kind of hit that occurred outside Mallory's condo, but whoever the bad guys were, they'd have to find them first.

"He's going to help us," Alyssa murmured. "He seems like a good man."

"Yeah. We can trust him to do what's right." He looked anywhere but directly at her. "Why don't you try and get some rest?"

"I will if you will," Alyssa said softly.

"Shouldn't be a problem, I'm going on less than four hours of sleep. I'll be fine."

She looked at him oddly for a long moment before slipping off the bed and retreating through the open connecting door. "Good night, Gage."

"Good night." Gage closed the door between their rooms, but didn't lock it. He headed for the bathroom, the hot water helping to relax the knotted muscles in his shoulders. He tried not to think of Dan's lifeless eyes staring at him from the office floor, but the image haunted him.

He must have dozed, because an odd noise had him jerking upright in surprise. He held his breath, his heart hammering in his chest. Was someone trying to break in?

Then he heard the noise again, from Alyssa's room. He softly padded to the connecting door and hesitantly opened it, waiting for his eyes to grow accustomed to the dim light. He was horrified to find Alyssa standing in front of her motel room door, struggling to unlock it as she mumbled under her breath.

He froze, trying to make sense of what he was seeing. Was she sleepwalking? "Alyssa? Where are you going?"

She didn't seem to hear him. "Blood—there's too much blood."

That was the same thing she'd said in the office after he'd stumbled over Dan's body. Was she dreaming about it now?

"Alyssa." He raised his voice and crossed over to place a hand on her shoulder. He gently tried to pry her away from the door. "Wake up. You're having a bad dream."

Either his voice or his touch must have gotten through to her, because she stopped struggling. She stood stock-still before turning to glance at him.

"Gage? What happened?"

The expression in her eyes made his heart thunder in his chest. She was looking up at him as if she recognized him. Did she finally remember?

The way he'd proposed marriage? And the way she'd broken up with him? He reined in his emotions with an effort. "I'm here," he murmured soothingly, brushing a strand of hair away from her damp cheek. "Come away from the door. You're safe, Alyssa."

"I don't remember getting up," she confessed softly. She shivered and he put a supporting arm around her shoulders. He wasn't prepared for her to cling to him, burying her face in the hollow of his chest.

"Alyssa," he murmured helplessly, running a soothing hand down her back. When she lifted her head and glanced up at him, he couldn't stop himself from capturing her mouth in a sweet kiss.

SEVEN

Her mouth was warm, pliant beneath his. Kissing Alyssa reminded him of the good times they'd had together and how much he cared about her. But as much as he wanted to crush her close and deepen the kiss, he forced himself to ease away.

Alyssa stared up at him, her eyes dazed. "You shouldn't have done that," she whispered, lifting a hand to her mouth.

"I'm sorry," he said, accepting full responsibility for his actions. She was right—he shouldn't have kissed her like that. As if they were still a couple, when he knew full well they weren't.

"You don't even know for sure I'm Alyssa!" Her voice held a note of panic.

"I know you're Alyssa," he said soothingly. "But if you don't believe me, take a look in the mirror. Half your rose and dagger tattoo is missing."

"It is?" She scrambled from the bed, apparently anxious to see for herself. She spent what seemed like an inordinate amount of time in the bathroom before she returned. "You're right. This tattoo is fake. I guess I must be Alyssa."

He nodded and stood, giving her plenty of room to get back into bed. "I'm glad you finally know who you are."

"I already told you that knowing isn't remembering. I don't remember who I am, and I don't remember you, Gage," she said in a low anguished tone. "I wish I did, but I don't."

"I know." He tried to smile reassuringly, realizing that by kissing her he'd just ruined the perfect opportunity to start their relationship over. "I didn't mean to take advantage of the situation, Alyssa. I only came over because you were having a nightmare."

"Yes. I remember dreaming about blood." She shivered and clenched her hands together tightly as if to keep them from shaking. "Lots of blood."

"Don't force your memory," he advised, wishing he could do something to ease her torment. "The doctor told you it would return when you're ready."

"I think I'm a little afraid to remember," she admitted in a low whisper. "What if the blood from my dream is real? What if I saw something horrible?"

His heart twisted at the stark anguish in her eyes. "Don't think about your dream any more tonight.

For now, I want you to rest. You're safe, Alyssa. I won't let anything happen to you."

"Thanks, Gage." She offered a faint smile. "I'm sorry I woke you. I'm sure I'll be fine now. Good night."

"Good night, Alyssa." He didn't think she'd really be able to go back to sleep, but he sensed she needed to be alone. Thanks to his impatience, she needed space.

Time and distance far away from him.

Alyssa could hear Gage moving softly around in his connecting room. Ridiculous to feel a sense of loss, considering he was right next door.

Her lips still tingled from his kiss. And if she were honest with herself, she'd admit that Gage's kiss had felt a little familiar, almost like coming home. She closed her eyes, willing her evasive memories to return. But there was only the infernal swirling mist.

If she was really Alyssa, then it was no wonder she was so attracted to Gage. But it wasn't just that he was handsome, in a rugged sort of way. She liked what she knew about him so far. He believed in God, which was important to her. He was also polite, considerate and protective. All very positive and admirable qualities. So why couldn't she remember him?

Her head began to throb, so she closed her eyes and concentrated on breathing. Maybe she didn't have specific and distinct memories about Gage, but she instinctively trusted him. She believed he'd protect her. Hadn't she felt safe with him the first time she met him? Back at the hospital, when everyone thought she was Mallory?

The danger surrounding them was all too real. The bullets that had rained around them had been real. Dan's dead body with the knife protruding from his chest had been real. She was convinced her fear of Officer Crane was real, too.

She felt so helpless. Useless. How could she help Gage if she couldn't remember what she was so afraid of? Instinctively, a Bible verse from 2 Samuel flashed in her mind, so clearly it was as if she could see the words on the page. *It is God who arms me with strength and keeps my way secure.*

Alyssa closed her eyes and opened her heart to prayer. *Dear Lord, please give me strength. Guide me and help me to remember. Amen.*

Gage tossed and turned, unable to get comfortable. He still felt guilty for kissing Alyssa. No matter how she'd turned to him when she was afraid, the last thing she needed was for him to crowd her.

Patience, an admirable quality, had always been

difficult for him. Alyssa had told him to pray to God for patience. He didn't have the heart to tell her he doubted praying to God would change his basic personality.

But he could believe that God was testing him. And finding him less than worthy. Guilt, his new constant companion, tightened his chest. He should have told Alyssa the truth about their broken engagement. In the beginning, when he'd thought that she was Mallory, he'd alluded to a relationship between them. He hadn't come out and claimed to be Alyssa's boyfriend, but he also hadn't corrected her obvious assumption.

Now their relationship, or lack thereof, was like a giant elephant in the room. He decided to tell her first thing in the morning. Alyssa should know the truth.

Clearly, Alyssa had been right all along. Hidden land mines of danger surrounded the Jefferson project. But he couldn't comprehend why. Who else, besides Hugh Jefferson, would benefit from building the Riverside Luxury Condos? And why kill City Councilman Ray Schaefer? Had the councilman's death been a necessary evil, as Dan's must have been? A way to silence them so they couldn't betray the truth?

The truth about *what?*

Gage tried to ignore the endless fountain of

questions. But no matter how hard he tried, he couldn't seem to push them aside long enough to fall asleep.

Loud, insistent pounding startled him from his thought. Gage staggered to his feet and headed for the door. Peering through the peephole, he recognized Jonah. The light outside their room must have burned out. He could barely make out his friend's grim features in the early-dawn light.

"Gage?" Alyssa's voice called out from behind the door to her room. She must not have been sleeping, either.

"It's Jonah." Gage undid the locks and opened the door, glancing at his watch. Not quite six yet. He stifled a yawn. "Hey, thanks for coming back. Did you find out anything?"

"Yeah." Jonah shouldered past him and quickly shut the door. A sharp tingle of fear slithered down Gage's spine when Jonah shot the dead bolt home and rechained the lock on the door. Jonah wasn't afraid of anything, but he certainly wasn't taking any chances now.

"What is it?" Gage didn't like the grim expression on Jonah's face. Jonah snagged the chair he'd used earlier, and Alyssa reclaimed her spot on the bed, hugging her knees, her gaze darting between the two of them.

"It's bad." Jonah ran a hand over his haggard features. "Worse than I'd expected." Jonah looked as if he hadn't slept a wink, and Gage immediately felt bad for sending his friend out to face Dan's death alone. But he couldn't have left Alyssa, either.

"You'd better tell me," Gage said, mentally bracing himself as he dropped into the vacant chair.

"The cops were already at your office building when I arrived."

Gage blinked and straightened. "What? How could they know about Dan? We didn't report his death. We didn't call anyone but you."

Jonah lifted red-rimmed eyes to meet his. "I'm telling you, they were already there. Gave me some baloney about how they'd gotten an anonymous tip that they'd felt compelled to follow up on. They wanted to know why I was there."

Fear churned in his gut. The situation was getting worse by the minute. "What did you tell them?"

"That you and I are friends and that you'd called me because you hadn't heard from your project manager. That I'd promised to do a little digging to see if I could find the guy on my own time."

A dizzy wave of relief washed over him. "So they bought your story."

"Possibly, but I wouldn't bank on it. Your pal, Officer Crane, was there." Jonah glanced at Alyssa.

"He's part of this. I knew it," she whispered.

Gage noticed that this time, Jonah didn't argue. "They'd just started to record the crime scene when I arrived. I tried to claim the case as my own, but Crane told me that the case already belonged to Detective Sean Foley. I hung around until they were finished." He sighed heavily. "They want to talk to you, Gage. I promised to bring you in."

No way. He wasn't going anywhere. This is exactly what they wanted. To tie him up in red tape until he was rendered helpless, so they could get to Alyssa. He refused to leave her alone and vulnerable.

"After finishing up at the crime scene, I went back to my office," Jonah continued. "I thought I'd try to look into the Jefferson project. You know, review the problems they had getting it approved."

"And?" Gage held his breath.

"And nothing. I hit a brick wall." Jonah frowned and dragged his gaze up to meet Gage's. "You know computers are my thing. Remember when we were seventeen and I hacked into the government system?"

Gage nodded.

"Not this time. I can't tell you how many layers of security I went through. There's something odd about this Jefferson guy." Jonah scowled. "Why would the roots of a condo project be buried in security deeper than Fort Knox?"

Gage shook his head, unable to speak. Whatever the secret was, he knew that people had died because of it.

And Alyssa's memory held the key.

Alyssa couldn't get warm. She'd cranked the heat unit in the corner of the dingy motel room, yet she couldn't manage to get warm.

Your pal, Officer Crane, was there. The words echoed in her mind. She shivered and rubbed her arms. If the police were somehow part of the danger surrounding the Jefferson project, how high did the deception go? To the shift supervisor over Creepy Crane? To the chief of police? The mayor?

Her gaze settled on Jonah. He and Gage shared an easy camaraderie, but what if the detective wasn't entirely innocent? He was a cop. And he'd promised to bring Gage in for questioning. A shiver racked her body. Maybe Jonah was a good cop doing his job. She prayed Gage's instincts were right. They couldn't fight the entire Milwaukee Police Department or the myriad of city government officials on their own.

"We need to get out of town." She hadn't realized she'd spoken out loud until Gage and Jonah swung their gazes in her direction. Determination made her raise her chin. "You can't take Gage in—

they'll try to pin Dan's death on him. At least long enough to distract us from the Jefferson project."

"Don't worry, I'm not going anywhere. I won't leave you alone." Gage's tone was lined with velvet steel. Overwhelming relief filled her heart. No matter what may have transpired between them, he still cared. Which was good, because heaven knew, she cared about him, too.

"If you take off, you'll look guilty," Jonah warned. "They can't pin this on you—the scene was set up to look like a robbery."

"Unless my prints are conveniently found on the knife," Gage argued.

"Too obvious. And since you found him, your prints could be explained." Jonah didn't relent.

"But they don't know I was there. I left the scene."

Jonah shrugged. "You had a hysterical female on your hands, what else could you do?"

Alyssa's cheeks burned and she hid her face against her knees. As much as she wanted to protest, she really had been one step away from hysteria. How could she explain the sense of danger that haunted her? Had the police gotten there right after they left? What if she and Gage had still been there? Would there have been three bodies lying on the office floor? She shivered again. The image of Dan's body was still embedded in her mind.

"They're not going to buy that, and even if they did I don't care. I'm not leaving Alyssa alone. Not for a second." Gage's voice jerked her thoughts away from the morbid.

"Okay, okay. Let me think for a minute." Jonah scowled and nearly swayed in his seat. "If they're really trying to set you up, then we need to take your statement sooner than later. But in a controlled way. Maybe you need a lawyer."

A lawyer? Alyssa's stomach tightened and fear threatened to choke her. They were in serious trouble if Jonah was recommending a lawyer.

"Maybe we need to find Mallory," Gage said.

"Mallory?" Jonah's head snapped up. "Why?"

Gage shifted restlessly in his seat. "Alyssa left a message on Mallory's answering machine saying it was urgent they talk. Alyssa sounded afraid, but we don't know what happened after that. But what if she had a brief conversation with Mallory? Could be Mallory knows something that will help steer us in the right direction."

"Any idea where to look for her?" Jonah asked.

Gage sighed and shook his head. "I went to Alyssa's town house, but she wasn't there. And the place was completely empty, as if Alyssa had closed the place down before she left. And Mallory wasn't at her condo, either."

"I wouldn't have put Mallory in danger," Alyssa spoke up, causing both men to look at her. "If I was in danger, I would warn Mallory to be careful. To get away and hide. I doubt she knows anything that can help us."

The blunt comment left a strained silence among the group. Finally Jonah rose to his feet. "I really should force you to come in for questioning."

Gage tensed, hands balled into fists at his sides. Alyssa knew he wasn't going anywhere. "You can try."

Jonah let out a disgusted sigh. "Forget it. You're right. This whole thing reeks of an inside job. I don't blame you for wanting to take off. But you need to stay in touch with me, Gage. I mean it. I can't work this thing in the dark."

Alyssa breathed easier when Jonah relented. She was so glad he wasn't going to force Gage to go in. But where did that leave them? What should they do next?

"Jonah, maybe you shouldn't work this thing at all." Gage's voice was soft, and her heart squeezed at the flash of concern reflected in his eyes. "I don't want any more of my friends turning up dead. Maybe you should just turn and walk away. Pretend you never found me."

"Are you going to leave it alone?" Jonah countered. "Are you going to turn around and walk away?"

"No." There was no hesitation in Gage's tone. "But I don't have a choice. Alyssa's life is in danger."

She stared at him in exasperation. "Your life is in danger now, too, Gage."

"She's right, you're both in danger." Jonah grimaced. "And you know me well enough to know I won't walk away, either. God will watch over us. Just be sure to stay in touch, understand?"

"Yeah, I hear you." Gage stood and followed Jonah toward the door and then held out his hand. "I owe you again, Jonah. More than I'll ever be able to repay."

"You don't owe me anything," Jonah corrected softly. "This is what friends are for." He took Gage's outstretched hand and shook it firmly. "Keep me informed if you stumble across any new information." He dropped Gage's hand then shot a sidelong glance at Alyssa. "Or if Alyssa's memory returns."

"I'd like to go back to my office. See if Dan left anything in his notes that might clue us in as to what he might have found."

Jonah shook his head. "Don't bother. The cops took all of the paperwork in as evidence. I'm sure you won't find anything left that's any use to you."

Paperwork? Evidence of a robbery? That didn't make any sense. Her stomach tightened with dread. The cops were one step ahead of them every time. Jonah was right. If Creepy Crane was involved in this, there wouldn't be a shred of evidence left behind. He would have made sure of it.

"Dan was more than my chief project manager, he was my friend," Gage argued.

"Trust me, I'm not about to let a dirty cop tarnish my badge." Jonah was no less fierce. "But we need to tread carefully. Don't do anything until you hear from me."

Gage let out a deep, frustrated sigh. "Okay, I'll wait to hear from you."

"Good. You should probably find a new place to stay tonight, just to be on the safe side. I'm using my private car and made sure I wasn't followed, but it doesn't hurt to be extra careful. Especially since we know someone on the inside is involved in this."

"Sounds like a good plan," Alyssa said, getting up and walking over to stand beside Gage. The fog still clouded her memory, but the sense of urgency was back in full force. She had the distinct impression there was something important she needed to do. But what?

Jonah opened the door, but then paused and turned back to Gage. "Call my cell when you get settled in your new digs."

"I will."

Jonah left, closing the door behind him. She turned back to find her duffel bag. They needed to find a safe haven.

If such a thing even existed.

Gage disappeared into his room, no doubt to collect his own things. There was an abrupt pounding on the motel door, and her heart leaped into her throat.

"Wait!" Gage was there in an instant. He moved toward the doorway and took a moment to peer through the peephole. "Jonah?" He quickly opened the door. "What's wrong?"

"You need to get out of here! A Milwaukee squad car just pulled in and I have a bad feeling they're looking for you."

EIGHT

Gage didn't question Jonah's instincts, because he suspected the same thing. And even if they weren't looking for them, he wasn't about to take a chance, not with Alyssa's life. He took her duffel along with his and tossed them over his shoulder. Clutching Alyssa's hand firmly, he followed Jonah outside.

Red and blue flashing lights pinpointed the squad car located half a dozen parking slots away from his truck. There was no sign of the officers. Were they inside grilling the clerk? How had they found him so quickly? By putting an APB out on his truck tag?

"Take my wheels." Jonah must have had the same thought as he shoved a set of keys into Gage's hand. "It's the green Bronco at the end of the row."

Gage quickly palmed the keys and tossed his set to Jonah. They didn't have much time. The officers could come out of the tiny lobby at any moment.

Keeping close to the wall, Gage jogged toward the Bronco with Alyssa right beside him. Just as he opened the door, he heard a shout.

"Stop! Police!"

"Hurry!" Gage tossed the bags inside and jumped behind the wheel. He jammed the key into the ignition and started the vehicle as Alyssa scrambled into the seat beside him. She managed to pull the passenger door closed when he threw the Bronco into Reverse and floored it. A brief glance toward the motel confirmed the cops were high-tailing it back to their squad car. He didn't doubt they intended to give chase.

"They're following." Alyssa voiced his thoughts. "Step on it, Gage."

He didn't argue. The Bronco roared beneath his touch. As he maneuvered the city streets he shifted through his options. Where could they go? The cops on their tail had no doubt called for backup. With no thought beyond getting out of the city, he took a wild turn and headed for the interstate. "Buckle your seat belt."

"You, too," she pointed out as she fastened hers then twisted in her seat to peer out the back window.

Gage kept his eyes glued to the road as he tried to fasten his seat belt one-handed. She reached across his chest to help him. "Keep your head down," he ordered. Wrestling with the steering wheel, he took another sharp turn. A few more blocks and they'd be on the interstate. "For all we know they're trigger-happy."

Alyssa ignored him, turning again in her seat to stare behind them. "They lost some ground on that last turn."

What was she doing? He didn't want a play-by-play from her. He needed Alyssa to stay safe. That's all he'd ever wanted, to protect her from the seedy side of life. In spite of all his efforts, though, they were hip-deep in sludge now. To throw the cops off, he drove over the median to the wrong side of the street then made a quick turn. Thankfully the traffic wasn't too bad at this hour on a Sunday morning, although several cars honked at him in warning. If he remembered correctly, there was another on-ramp for the interstate a few blocks down.

"Come on," he muttered as he swerved around a slow-moving vehicle. "Almost there."

"Hey, now they're really far back." Alyssa sounded relieved.

"How far?" Despite his need to keep his eyes on the road, he risked a glance in the rearview mirror. The squad behind him had picked up a second squad, and he was glad to see they'd dropped farther behind.

"Keep going, Gage. We're going to make it," she said encouragingly.

Alyssa's positive attitude shocked him. He'd expected her to fall apart, but instead she was supporting him. Even though they were breaking the law.

"Look out!" Alyssa cried.

He swerved sharply, just in time to avoid a truck that had pulled out in front of him. His heart leaped into his throat. Focus. He needed to focus. And to pray.

Dear God, help us. Keep us safe!

"Hang on." Gage sped up the on-ramp. "And keep your head down!" One of the cars started to move forward and he took a path around it, effectively cutting it off. The driver laid on the horn in annoyance.

Once on the freeway, he quickly sliced through three lanes of traffic to reach the far-left lane. Gage knew they couldn't stay on the interstate for long. There would be new cops on their tail in no time. He was certain every cop within a fifty-mile radius had been alerted to search for Jonah's Bronco.

Still, he waited until they'd gone a good couple of miles before he swerved onto the narrow left shoulder and slammed on the brakes.

Alyssa squealed and hung on to the dashboard. "What are you doing?"

Gage wrenched the wheel into an illegal U-turn in the middle of the interstate. Once he'd gained enough speed, he cut across the three lanes of traffic and took the first exit. At the end of the ramp he turned right, then at the next street he hung another quick left, all the while heading south.

"You did it, Gage." Alyssa's voice was full of awed relief. "You lost them."

Adrenaline surged through his bloodstream even though he knew they weren't safe. Not yet. He glanced at Alyssa. "I'm sorry if I scared you."

She actually smiled. "Yeah, I wouldn't recommend running from the police often, but I'd rather be safe."

"And we are. For now." He was impressed she'd taken his stunt-driving so well. "But we have to ditch the car."

She paled. "You're not going to steal one, are you?"

"No. Don't worry, that's not part of the plan."

She visibly relaxed. "But you do have a plan, right?"

He wished he did. Somehow, they needed to lose themselves in the city. Milwaukee was a big place. Shouldn't be too difficult to hide. He pulled into a well-known shopping mall parking lot and threw the vehicle into Park. "Sort of a plan. One that starts with leaving Jonah's Bronco here and going forward on foot."

Alyssa did her best to keep up with Gage, and the adrenaline from their wild car ride had sustained her for a while. But after two hours of walking, her legs felt as if each limb weighed a hundred pounds. Her head and ankle throbbed in unison and her throat was parched. She'd give anything for a long, cold drink of water.

With both their bags slung over his shoulder, Gage led the way through another parking lot, around a building and then through a back alley. She didn't voice a single complaint. Gage seemed to know what he was doing. He'd lost the cops on their tail and stayed off the main streets where they could easily be picked up.

"There's a bus stop ahead," Gage murmured close to her ear. "We'll hop the bus for a few blocks then try to head farther south."

"Where are we going?" She didn't like feeling as if they were stumbling around in the dark. Nothing about their surroundings seemed familiar. The street signs were a meaningless blur. She tried to remain calm, in spite of the mist that continued to swirl in her mind. Clouds obliterated the sun from overhead. Despite the warm air and her exhaustion, she shivered. Danger could be anywhere, around the next corner, over the next hill. How would she know?

"We're only a few miles from the Jefferson construction site."

"What?" She stumbled. Gage grabbed her elbow to prevent her from falling forward. She pushed away a blond curl that stuck to her sweaty cheek. "Tell me you're not serious."

"I'm very serious." He tugged her to the right. She forced her confused and exhausted feet to follow. Her ankle screamed in protest. Belatedly she noticed the blue bus stop sign.

"Don't you think that's the first place they'll look?" She couldn't quite grasp his logic.

"Maybe. But it's also where Dan was when I called him to ask about the Jefferson project." Gage sat on the bus stop bench and Alyssa dropped gratefully beside him.

"So?"

"So if there's anything left at the site that might indicate what's going on, I want to find it before the police do." Gage's gaze was grim.

"I see." He was right. They wouldn't get to the bottom of this mess unless they had something to go on. Swallowing her apprehension, she stretched out her legs, gently moving her sore ankle.

Gage picked up a newspaper someone had left on the bench and held it up to shield their faces.

"Are you okay?" Gage asked in a low voice, as if sensing her bone-weary exhaustion.

"Fine," she murmured. She stared at the small newspaper print directly in front of her face. Would reading the news trigger her memory? She scanned a few articles.

A story about the new mayoral candidate caught her eye and she shifted a bit so she could read it easier. There'd been a benefit the night before last, and a large picture of two men shaking hands at the Pfister Hotel was splashed on the front page. She quickly bypassed the picture in her haste to read the article. The reporter reiterated how the incumbent Mayor Flynn had suffered an unexpected heart attack and died several weeks ago. Eric Holden was the Common Council president who'd stepped up to the role as interim mayor. Holden was also the favorite candidate to date. Early polls showed him in a wide lead over former City Councilman Gerald Maas.

She thought the name Holden seemed a little familiar. Their bus pulled up. "Let's go," Gage said, setting the newspaper aside.

Alyssa took the newspaper and folded it, keeping it so she could look at the article again later. Interesting how she didn't remember her family or her friends, but a stranger's name stirred a shadow in the misty fog of her brain.

Gage stayed back, allowing her to step into the bus first. She slid onto a cracked vinyl seat, scooting over to the window to make room for Gage. Once they were seated, the bus lumbered down the street.

"You're sure about going to the building site?" she asked. "You don't think the police will be there waiting for you?"

"It's possible they think they have whatever they need from my office building." Gage glanced at her, concern in his eyes. "But I can always get a room at a motel first, and you can wait for me there."

"No. I'm going with you." Despite the warmth, she was cold, inside and out. She was afraid of going to the Jefferson condo building site, but she was even more afraid of Gage going off without her. What if something happened to him? Then she'd really be all alone.

"Okay, if you're sure."

"I'm sure." They needed to stick together, now more than ever. She'd do whatever was necessary to prevent Gage from ending up like Dan Kirkland.

Dead.

"Gage? Have I been here before?" she whispered from their crouched position beside the trailer office site. The newspaper worked its way out of her bag, and she tucked it firmly inside, so it wouldn't blow away in the breeze, giving away their position.

"No, we only just started building here within the past month or so." Gage swept the area with his gaze, presumably to make sure the police hadn't beat them to the scene.

She found that bit of information strange. Why wouldn't she have come here? Wouldn't she have been interested in what her boyfriend was doing?

"Stay here," Gage murmured. "I'm heading inside."

She grabbed his arm before he could make his move. "Without me?"

"Alyssa, I need you to stay here, to keep an eye out for the police." His gaze pleaded with her to understand. "I promise I won't be long."

She wanted to protest. To make him listen. But he was right in that someone needed to keep watch. Besides, in the bright light of day, carrying two duffel bags holding their meager belongings, they were too noticeable together. Her stomach clenched but she forced herself to release his arm.

"Okay, but if you're not back in fifteen minutes, I'm coming to find you," she threatened.

His cinnamon-colored eyes widened with alarm. "Fifteen minutes isn't much time. Just be patient and keep watch. If you see anything suspicious get somewhere safe, okay?"

She frowned. Did Gage really think she'd leave him to face the danger alone? If so, he didn't know her very well. She'd appreciated his protectiveness, but now it seemed he was carrying it a bit too far. "Come back out here in fifteen minutes to let me know how it's going. Don't shut me out, Gage. We're in this together."

He stared at her for a long moment but then gave a curt nod. "Okay, fifteen minutes." Before she could say anything more, he disappeared around the corner of the trailer.

She let her breath out in a soundless sigh. Once they were safe, she needed to have a little heart-to-heart with Gage. They couldn't argue like this every time they faced some sort of danger. Though her memory was a temporary blank, she could still function as part of the team. Even with her hurt ankle, she hadn't complained or slowed them down so far, had she?

Steadily, she inched forward until she could see around the corner of the trailer. Gage was nowhere in sight, so she assumed he was already inside. Would he find the evidence they so desperately needed? She prayed he would.

With a glance at her watch, she settled on top of the duffel bags to wait. There was no way she was going to give him a second longer than the time frame they'd agreed upon. She stared at her watch, as if she could will the hands to move faster.

Fourteen minutes, thirty-five seconds and counting.

Gage used his master key to open the door to the trailer/office and stepped inside. Luckily, it was Sunday, and as he'd expected, there wasn't anyone inside working. He moved toward the desk he or Dan would use whenever they were on-site. There was a tall, old beat-up file cabinet next to the desk. He opened drawers and began looking through paperwork, hoping he'd recognize the clue when he found it.

What information could Dan have stumbled on? Most of the files were neatly organized, except in the last drawer he found one sticking up, as if it had been hastily returned.

The original bid on the Jefferson project.

Gage didn't hesitate to pull the fat file out and lay it on the desk. He scanned the information inside. His signature stared up at him from the original quotes, but then he saw there were additional notes scribbled in the margins. Examining them closer, he realized the handwriting was Dan's.

"MaKay Builders, Conrath Construction Company, Jacobson and Sons." He read the names of his largest competitors out loud. There were numbers written alongside the names. It took him a minute to realize they were quotes.

Two of the three quotes were a little lower than his winning bid.

For a moment he could only stare at the information with a sense of disbelief. That couldn't be right. Why would Jefferson give the deal to a small construction company like Drummond Builders if it had won the lowest bid? He stared at the scribbled notes in the margin. Had he read them wrong? Were the numbers something other than dollar amounts? At the bottom of the notations was a strange reference to Northwestern University.

Before he could make sense out of that, the wail of sirens split the air. Reacting instinctively, he slammed the folder shut and jumped from the chair. Tucking the folder under his arm, he peered out the closest window. The knot in his gut tightened.

He couldn't see Alyssa from this angle, but the police seemed as if they were definitely headed this way. He never should have left her alone outside without a cell phone. She was vulnerable, more so with the void in her memory. He was responsible for her. If he didn't move fast, they'd be trapped.

Fifty-two seconds to go. What was taking Gage so long? Had he found something that would help them? A full minute had passed since the guy had wandered too close to the construction site for her peace of mind. The stranger was a big guy, dressed in baggy jeans and faded T-shirt, and she'd watched in horror as he'd paused barely two feet from her hiding place to light a cigarette. Was he someone from Jefferson's payroll sent to find her and Gage? Frightened beyond belief, she stayed motionless. And when her nose had twitched at the scent of smoke, she'd pinched her nostrils, fighting the urge to sneeze. He'd stood smoking for agonizingly long moments then flicked his partially finished butt into a drum that functioned as a garbage can. Luckily, he'd wandered away, back toward the other side of the construction site.

Thirty seconds. Tired of waiting, she crept from her hiding place and then froze when she heard sirens, her heart hammering in her throat. Almost instantly, she saw the red and blue flashing lights in the distance that seemed to be headed straight for them.

No! The police had found them!

NINE

As Gage eased out from the trailer, he was assaulted by the acrid scent of smoke. He couldn't see what was burning, but a small cloud of smoke drifted over from the other side of the trailer. Keeping flat against the aluminum siding so the police couldn't see him, he went around to the back, where he'd left Alyssa.

She wasn't there. His heart leaped into his throat as he scanned the area searching for her. Where was she? Had she run because of the police cars? He found himself hoping she had.

Ka-boom!

The ground shook and he stumbled over the duffel bags near his feet, nearly falling flat on his face. Where in the world was Alyssa? He peered around the corner toward the front of the trailer, horrified to see a squad car was pulling up into the driveway in front of the trailer. Two cops jumped out, but instead of going inside the trailer, they ran off toward the source of the smoke.

"Gage? Let's go!"

Shocked, he spun around to see Alyssa crouched behind him. The pungent scent of gasoline and smoke permeated her clothes. "Are you okay? Did you start a fire?"

She flushed and nodded guiltily. "I'm pretty sure the pickup truck was abandoned. It was rusted through and all four tires were flat. Let's go, we have to hurry!"

He wasn't going to argue, since the two officers were preoccupied by the fire. "This way," he whispered. He grabbed the two duffel bags and urged her to go first so he could protect her from behind.

They left the shelter of the trailer and, staying low, crept behind the police cars to get away from the construction site. Crossing the street was their biggest risk, and when Alyssa veered to the right, toward the parking structure about a block down, he followed her lead.

Her choice was a stroke of genius. Soon they were hidden within the dim interior of the structure, shielded by the myriad of parked cars. Silently, they wove through the rows to the other side. Alyssa didn't hesitate but climbed up and over the waist-high wall, landing with a muffled grunt on her feet on the other side. Gage couldn't help but grin with admiration. She was smart, constantly thinking even when running for their lives. He tossed the duffels over the low wall and then followed her to the other side. Although she'd taken twenty years off his life back there, he couldn't deny her idea for a diversion saved them.

Still, from here on out, he wasn't going to keep exposing her to danger. He wasn't a cop like Jonah, but all those years on the move with his dad had taught him how to fend for himself. He'd wanted to protect Alyssa from the seedy side of life. She was a nurse, not a private investigator.

They kept moving, cutting through streets and taking alleys whenever possible. Gage tried to focus on his surroundings. They needed a plan. They couldn't keep running around the city on foot. "Take a left here," he said. "There's a college campus just a few blocks down, with lots of students hanging around. We need to be someplace where we'll blend in."

She arched a brow. "Are you saying I look like a college student?"

He flashed a tired smile. "The way we're dressed, we both could pass for students." He paused to glance at her gas-stained sweatpants. "Did you really blow up a truck?"

"I wasn't trying to blow it up," Alyssa defended herself. "I was trying to set the seats on fire, but that didn't work. I wasn't even sure there was any gas in the tank, but I stuck the oily rag with the cigarette butt into the opening and ran. I was just as surprised as anyone when the thing exploded."

A flash of fear gripped his chest. "You're lucky you weren't killed," he said, unable to keep his voice from rising. "You should have stayed put like I told you to!"

She frowned and tucked a stray curl behind her ear. "You know, Gage, you're not giving me enough credit. I helped save us back there. The least you could do is to thank me, rather than giving me a lecture."

He was taken aback by her tone. "I wasn't giving you a lecture. Don't you understand? I need to know you're safe."

"Neither of us is safe," she argued heatedly. "The way you want to protect me is sweet, but we're in this together. You need to treat me as an equal partner, Gage, instead of a liability."

Equal partner? She had to be joking. She couldn't remember her name, much less anything that might lead them to the source of danger. His job was to keep her safe. End of discussion. "You're not a liability," he said, trying to smooth things over. He absolutely didn't want her to feel bad. This was his fault for not listening to her in the first place. Clearly time to change the subject. "Let's go down this street here. There's a pub called Rickey's where we can sit for a while and get something to eat."

As it was the end of August, the impending fall semester had brought many students back to campus. Rickey's wasn't overly crowded, but there were enough people that they could fade into the crowd. Gage pushed through the students gathered at the bar to watch the baseball game on the dual televisions mounted overhead. He was grateful to find a small table in the back corner.

Alyssa dropped into the chair with a low moan. "My aching feet," she murmured.

During their months together, Alyssa would often come home after a long shift in the E.R. complaining about her sore feet. He'd always offered to give her foot massages to relieve the pressure and pain. He missed those days they'd spent together. Going out for brunch after church on the weekends she had off work. Spending Saturday evenings down at Jazz in the Park near the lakefront. They'd spent a lot of time together. What had gone so wrong?

A waitress came over to their table to ask if they'd like something to drink. "Would you mind bringing a pitcher of ice water and a couple of glasses?" Alyssa asked. "I'm really thirsty."

The waitress narrowed her gaze, as if perturbed

at the lack of a sale. Gage spoke up hastily. "Would you also bring menus? We'd like to order something to eat."

Her scowl eased and the waitress nodded. "I'll be right back."

"How much cash do you have?" Alyssa asked in a low voice. "I'm hungry, but maybe we should limit our meals."

"We're fine," he assured her. In reality he had only a couple of hundred in cash, but he didn't want her to worry. If nothing else, he could use an ATM machine, but he was sure that the MPD would be trying to track them by watching their transactions, so he'd have to use one on the opposite end of the city. Not an easy feat without a set of wheels.

"If you're sure," Alyssa murmured, taking the glossy menu from the waitress. "Ooh, grilled chicken sounds wonderful."

He had to smile, because she always ordered grilled chicken. He used to tease her about it.

He remembered everything about Alyssa. The way she brushed and braided her long hair, the way she smelled like lilacs after the rain, the way she used to smile at him, as if they'd shared a deep secret. And then the day she'd given him back his ring, stating she couldn't marry him.

"Gage?" she called, breaking into his thoughts. "What do you want to eat?"

"Oh, uh, a medium burger with fries," he said quickly, barely glancing at the menu. Rickey's always had great burgers. "Thanks."

The waitress took their menus and hurried off. He took a long drink of his water while glancing at Alyssa. She looked tired, but her blue eyes sparkled. "So where do we go from here?" she asked.

Good question. "We need to find another cheap motel, but offhand I don't know of any and I don't want to be wandering around where we can be easily spotted."

She grimaced. "Well, I'm no help."

"Don't worry, I'll come up with something. Would be nice to have access to a computer so I could do a search."

"Maybe the university library is open," Alyssa suggested.

"Good idea," he murmured. Why hadn't he thought of that? "We'll head over there after we finish eating."

Their food arrived a few minutes later, and they both busied themselves with eating. They ate relatively quickly, since they hadn't eaten since the day before. On the television closest to them, he caught a glimpse of the Jefferson building site. With a frown, he stared at the screen. Alyssa must have noticed because she glanced over to see what had caught his attention.

Breaking News: Fire at Jefferson Construction Site was the main headline across the bottom of the screen. A TV reporter stood back as the cameraman panned the scene, and Gage noticed several fire trucks parked alongside the police cars.

"Here's a police officer now," the reporter said. "Officer, do you have any idea how this fire started?"

"We're still investigating, but we have reason to believe the cause is arson." The officer wasn't Aaron Crane, but Gage thought he caught a glimpse of the cop in the background. Didn't the guy ever sleep? Why was he at every single accident scene?

"Arson? This condo project was a source of contention in the recent mayoral debate between Maas and Holden. Maas has vocalized concerns related to the project. Do you think one of Maas's supporters is responsible for this?"

"We're not ruling anything out just yet, but we are looking for help in finding Gage Drummond and Mallory Roth. They are both persons of interest in regards to this fire and the unfortunate slaying of Daniel Kirkland. If anyone sees either of these people—" their pictures in full color were splashed on the screen "—please call our anonymous hotline as soon as possible."

He heard Alyssa suck in a harsh breath, and the burger curdled in his stomach. "Persons of interest" in his mind was akin to being set up to take the fall. All because someone thought they'd gotten too close to the truth behind the Jefferson project. Whatever the truth was.

"Let's go," he murmured, pulling out cash and leaving more than enough on the table to cover their tab. He reached for the duffel bags. "We need to get out of here."

Luckily she'd finished her grilled chicken. She spared a few minutes to finish her water before following Gage. What would they do now? Keep moving, obviously, but for how long? Thanks to this news story, the whole city would be looking for them. They'd have to stay out of public places. How could they figure out what was going on if they were constantly on the run?

Her ankle protested sharply when she matched her stride to keep up with Gage. Stubbornly, she ignored the pain. She suspected the injured tendons wouldn't heal very well unless she stayed off her foot, which wasn't going to happen anytime soon. No point in whining about what couldn't be changed.

She followed Gage to the back door of the bar. He seemed to know his way around, and they slipped outside without anyone stopping them. All they needed was a head start. "Are we still going to the library?" she asked.

"Yeah." He led the way across the street to the large university buildings. There was a group of kids standing out on the corner, and Gage asked them for directions to the library. They pointed them in the right direction.

The library was a large building, and Alyssa immediately felt safe among the stacks of books. She realized she loved libraries. Another memory? She glanced around, willing something to come to her, but no luck. She just knew she loved books.

As Gage used a computer to access the internet, she sat beside him, wondering once again about their relationship. Didn't she mind that he constantly tried to keep her safe? His protective attitude was nice and flattering, but at times she wanted to claw free of his cloak.

Gage was ruggedly attractive, but even more so, she was drawn to his musky, woodsy scent. She stared at his strong, square jaw and tried to remember being with him. She imagined her laughing expression from the photograph on Mallory's dresser. Had she felt happy with him? For a brief moment, she caught a flash of the two of them on a horse-and-buggy ride. A memory? Or just wishful thinking?

She wished she knew for sure.

"Okay, I found a place for us," Gage said. "It's about ten miles away, on the other side of town. Do you think you can make it that far?"

"Of course," she responded, although she wanted to wince. Ten miles? It would take hours to walk that far, unless Gage allowed them to take a bus part of the way. Risky to take the bus, although there weren't TVs in the city buses, so they might go undetected. Regardless, it wasn't as if they had much of a choice. She wished they could stay longer in the sanctuary of the library. "I wonder if Mallory sent me an email."

Gage swiveled to look at her. "Good idea. You have a Yahoo email account. Do you remember your password?" he asked eagerly.

"I can try a few that seem logical," she offered. Gage pulled up the Yahoo home page and typed in her email address. She took over at the keyboard, trying to think logically. What would she use as a password? Something with her nursing background? Gage's name? Mallory's?

She tried a few variations, but none of them worked. "I'm sorry, Gage." She hated feeling so helpless. Useless. If only she could remember.

"Don't worry—we can always try again later." He didn't show any sign of impatience. "But you gave me an idea. I'll check my email messages, too. Maybe Dan sent me something."

She leaned forward to read over his shoulder. "Did he?"

"No. Just a message from my dad, asking me to call him when I have time." Gage shut down the email program and turned to her. "Are you ready?"

"Sure." She stood, hiding a wince, and walked with Gage out of the library, back into the bright sunlight. From there, Gage took the lead, weaving a path on smaller, less traveled streets until he felt safe jumping on a bus.

Ten miles was a lot farther than what it sounded like, especially when they didn't take the direct route. And Gage had vetoed the bus idea. After what seemed like forever, but was really a few hours, they approached the motel.

"I need you to stay hidden until I've rented a room," Gage directed in a hushed tone. "I don't want them to see you, in case they're watching the news."

She wasn't sure she liked that idea. "What if they recognize you and call the police?" she asked.

"I'm going to use an assumed name and offer cash. Hopefully they won't insist on seeing an ID.

I'll ask for adjoining rooms." Gage glanced at her and shrugged. "Let's hope they don't ask any questions."

She swallowed hard and nodded. She could only hope and pray they didn't. "Okay. But hurry."

His expression softened. "I will."

The minutes went by agonizingly slowly, but soon she saw Gage come out of the motel office and walk down to a room on the end of the row. He unlocked the door and then gestured for her to come join him.

Inside, she saw he'd already opened the doors between the rooms. Almost immediately, Gage's phone rang. The noise made her jump. "It's Jonah," he said before answering. He listened for a minute and then said, "Yeah, we saw the news."

Listening to Gage's one-sided conversation left some gaps, but she caught the gist. "We didn't start the fire on purpose," he explained to Jonah. "The cops were coming and we used it as a diversion to get away. Don't shout—we had to go to the construction site, because I needed to know what Dan discovered. And I did find something interesting. My bid for the project wasn't the lowest one. There were two others that were slightly lower than mine. Granted, not by much, but it makes me think Jefferson specifically targeted Drummond Builders."

She glanced at him sharply. He hadn't said a

word to her about his discovery. Was he keeping secrets on purpose? To protect her? She'd tried to get him to understand they were in this together, but clearly, Gage preferred keeping her in the dark, a fact she didn't appreciate one bit.

Had Hugh Jefferson really targeted Drummond Builders? And if so, why?

"I know it doesn't make sense," Gage continued. "But I found Dan's notes written in the margin. It could be the odd discovery he'd mentioned to me over the phone."

Once Gage was doing more listening than talking, she crossed over to her duffel and took out the part of the newspaper she'd kept. She'd used a good chunk of it to start the fire in the old abandoned truck, but she'd kept the section with the article related to the mayoral debate.

The name Eric Holden still bothered her. Why did it sound so familiar? Smoothing the newspaper on the small round table, she found the article and went back to the front page, where it started. There was a large photo, with two men standing and shaking hands. She stared intently at them, trying to see the details of their facial features. She estimated Eric Holden was in his early forties, a handsome man with perfectly groomed dark hair with just the barest hint of gray at his temples.

Holden was noticeably taller and younger than the man standing across from him.

Her gaze dropped to the caption beneath the photo, and her heart lurched when she realized that the other man in the photo was the infamous Hugh Jefferson. She stared at the grainy photo of Jefferson. He didn't look at all familiar, and she was immensely relieved that he wasn't the same man who was standing next to Mallory in the glossy photo she'd found in Mallory's dresser.

The sign on the podium identified the location of the photo as the Pfister Hotel. Parts of her memory were intact. She knew the Pfister was a luxurious hotel in the heart of Milwaukee. For a moment she thought of the rose-colored evening gown she'd found in Mallory's condo. Had Mallory worn the gown to this benefit? The timing was certainly right. Had she been escorted by the man in the glossy photo? Or had she gone alone?

Gage finished up on the phone and came over to where she was intently studying the newspaper. "Did you find something?"

"Did you?" she countered, glancing up at him. "I heard you and Jonah talking about what you found in Dan's notes. Something about not being the lowest bid for the project?"

"Yes, that's correct." Gage was watching her

warily, as if sensing her discordant mood. "I guess I forgot to mention that when we were at Rickey's."

Maybe, or maybe he was trying to protect her again. She tried not to dwell on it. "Surely there are other reasons to choose a builder besides money. Maybe he liked your company's reputation?"

"Maybe," he said with a shrug. "But my company is so much smaller than the others that I can't believe my reputation is that much better. And there was a strange notation, too, about Northwestern University. I'm assuming Jefferson went there, but I haven't figured out why Dan thought it was significant. So what did you find?"

She tapped the glossy photo with a fingertip. "This is Eric Holden and Hugh Jefferson. According to the article, Jefferson is a huge supporter of Holden's campaign."

"That doesn't exactly surprise me," Gage admitted. "The two look very chummy in that picture."

"I found a rose-colored evening gown in Mallory's condo," she went on. "And look at this woman here, off to the side. All you can see is her back, but she has short blond hair and she's wearing a rose-colored gown. Do you think she could be Mallory? Do you think Mallory was actually at this benefit?" The moment she asked the question, an awful thought occurred to her.

What if the woman in the photo was really her,

Alyssa, dressed as Mallory? She'd taken Mallory's identity, and all along, they'd assumed she'd taken it to hide from danger. But what if she'd really taken Mallory's identity as a way to get information regarding Councilman Schaefer's death?

TEN

Gage stared at the photo, wishing he could see more than the woman's back. "This could be Mallory," he admitted. The pieces of the puzzle still didn't make much sense. Whether Mallory attended the benefit or not didn't help them much. He glanced at Alyssa and belatedly realized she'd gone pale. "What is it?" he asked in alarm. "Is something wrong?"

She slowly shook her head but didn't meet his gaze. "No, I'm fine."

He didn't believe her and found it agonizing to realize she didn't trust him enough to let him know what was going on in her mind. Was her lack of trust partially because he hadn't told her what he'd found inside the construction trailer? He hadn't been holding back on purpose. Truthfully, his priority had been to get Alyssa safely out of there. And then out of Rickey's when he saw their pictures splashed all over the news. He'd dragged her from one end of the city to the other, in spite of her sore ankle. It wasn't until he'd spoken to Jonah that he'd remembered what he'd found.

"Alyssa, I'm sorry."

She glanced up at him in surprise. "For what?"

He sank into a chair and spread his hands wide. "For making you feel bad. I'm not trying to keep information from you. We've been on the run since this morning, and when I see how exhausted you are, I can't help feeling guilty. This entire situation is mostly my fault. I would give anything to keep you safe."

Her smile was brittle. "Gage, I'm not going to break. I told you before, we're in this together. Rehashing what we could have done or should have done isn't going to help. We need to be focused on working through this, together. Through the good times and the bad."

She was asking too much of him. He didn't think he could survive if something happened to her. Didn't she understand they were in this mess only because he hadn't believed her? He stared down at his hands for a moment. "I promise to try," he said doubtfully.

There was a long moment of silence. "Do you mind if I ask you a question?"

"Anything," he answered readily.

"What kind of relationship did we have?" His

stomach clenched when her blue gaze captured his. "I mean, have we been dating for a long time? Were we serious?"

He'd figured she'd ask this question sooner rather than later. And he couldn't lie to her. "My feelings for you were serious," he admitted. "But you told me I didn't have a close enough relationship with God and that I was too overprotective."

"The overprotective part is easy to believe," she murmured dryly. "But I thought you told me you were a believer."

How could he explain what he didn't fully understand himself? "I do believe in God," he affirmed. "But I'm not as religious as you."

A small pucker furrowed her brow. "You don't pray?"

He thought about the few times over the past thirty-six hours he had prayed. For strength. For Alyssa's safety. To thank God for bringing her back into his life. He couldn't deny praying made him feel stronger. "Sometimes, yes. But probably not often enough. It's something I'm working on."

She tipped her head to the side. "Are you working on your faith for me or for yourself?"

He sucked in a quick breath, a lightbulb snapping on in the middle of his brain. When he'd met Alyssa, he'd renewed his faith for her sake, going to church, going to Bible study because that's what she'd wanted. But he hadn't taken his relationship with God to heart. Not as something he'd needed to do for himself. How could he have been such an idiot? "Yes, I won't lie to you. I was renewing my faith for you at first, but I've now realized I need to work on my faith for my own sake. And I really do want a closer relationship with God."

A small smile tugged on her mouth. "I'm glad. And if you need help, I'm here for you, Gage."

He wished he could hug her close, even kiss her. But he forced himself to keep his distance. He forced himself to look back at the newspaper photo. He wasn't a big fan of politics, but he sensed that Jefferson knew how to use them to his advantage. "We know there was discord among the city councilmen about Jefferson's condo project. Schaefer was against it, and so was the former mayor, but then he had a heart attack, and with Holden's help, the city approved Jefferson's permits. We started construction almost two weeks ago, so there has to be some reason Jefferson wanted to silence Schaefer, if we believe his claim he was stabbed by one of Jefferson's men."

"I'm with you so far," Alyssa urged.

Gage slowly shook his head. "I think Schaefer must have found something out about Jefferson. Jefferson must be involved in something illegal. It's the only thing that makes sense."

"And Jefferson has cops working for him, and the mayor on his side, to help cover up whatever illegal activity he's involved in," Alyssa added. "Could it have something to do with drugs?"

"I don't think so," he murmured. "Drugs don't fit. Has to be something related to the condo project. And the only thing I can think of is money laundering."

Alyssa gasped. "Gage! What if he's paying you to build his condos with dirty money?"

"I know." The very thought made him feel sick. "And that would explain why he wanted my company to do the work, even though we weren't the lowest bid. Could be he figured a smaller company wouldn't ask as many questions, or look too deeply into the source of his financing." And like a fool, he'd walked right into Jefferson's trap.

Alyssa grasped his hands in hers. "It's not too late, Gage. You can still get out of it."

He wished he had her confidence. "It's not going to be easy to break the contract. Not without losing my entire business. Besides, I have a feeling Jefferson is used to getting his way. He's not going to let me out of the contract easily. What we need is to find some sort of proof that we can use to go to the authorities."

"Going to the local police isn't going to help,"

she pointed out. "Not if Jefferson has them in his pocket."

He raised his grim gaze to meet hers. There had to be a way out of this mess. "Then I'll have no choice but to go to the FBI with whatever proof we find."

Alyssa yawned, trying to keep her eyes open. After being up so early and walking for so long, she could barely stay upright. She stretched out on top of the bed in her room while Gage made notes about their theory so far.

"Hi, Margaret, is Dad around?" she heard Gage ask. His voice was low, but she could hear through the open connecting doors.

She forced one eyelid open, glancing over to where Gage was using his cell phone to call his dad. Was Margaret his stepmother? She wished she knew more about Gage's past.

"He's golfing? Okay, just let him know I called. Thanks."

"Who's Margaret?" she asked.

"My dad's wife. I've met her a few times, she seems nice enough. She obviously cares about my dad." She noticed he avoided mentioning anything about his mother. "I'm going to head out to get some dinner for us. There's a fast-food restaurant a few blocks down the street."

She struggled to sit up. "I'll go with you."

"There's no need," he hastily assured her. "Why don't you stay here and take a nap?"

The idea of a nap had far too much appeal. But she refused to be treated like an invalid. "No way. Where you go, I go."

"Alyssa, please. Wait for me here. We're too noticeable together."

Here he went again, with his overprotective attitude. "Anyone can easily recognize you from your photo. We're both in danger, remember?"

"I look different with my stubbly face," he said, rubbing a hand over his beard. "And I don't think they'll look at me twice if I'm alone."

She put a hand up to her light hair. "Maybe I should get some hair dye?"

He stared at her, as if seriously considering her offer. "Might not be a bad idea," he admitted. "I'll look for a grocery store on the way. But please stay here, Alyssa. I gave Jonah our room number and he might try to swing by. I'd hate for him to come when neither of us is here."

She narrowed her gaze, hating how he'd boxed her in a corner. She didn't want Jonah to come here while they were both gone, either. "Okay, I'll wait here. But I expect you to be back in less than twenty minutes. I mean it, Gage, no going off on your own without me."

"I promise I'll be back in less than twenty minutes." He rose to his feet and strode toward the door. Then he stopped and glanced back over his shoulder. "What do you think of becoming a redhead?"

She hid her wince and nodded. "Sounds like a plan."

Gage flashed a quick grin and then eased out of the motel room door.

She must have dozed because when she woke up, Gage was sitting at the small table, munching a French fry. "I didn't want to wake you," he said by way of apology. "You looked as if you needed sleep more than food."

She grimaced and pushed her hair away from her face. "I suppose, but cold fries don't taste very good."

"I wrapped them in tinfoil to help keep them warm." He took out a burger and the foil-wrapped fries and handed them to her.

Burgers weren't on her list of top favorite foods, but right now she was so hungry she didn't care about the high fat content. Eagerly, she dug in. Even the lukewarm fries weren't too bad. "Have you heard from Jonah?" she asked between bites.

Gage nodded. "He texted me. He wants me to meet him at the fountain in Rainbow Park at nine."

"Nine? Tonight?" She glanced at her watch, surprised to see it was already seven-thirty. She'd slept later than she'd realized. "Why not come here?"

"He's afraid he'll be followed. He's already in trouble with his boss because we managed to escape from the motel earlier this morning. He doesn't want to let on that he's helping us."

The burger and fries she'd eaten congealed into a hard lump in the pit of her stomach. "Did he get arrested?"

"No, but apparently they threatened to. They took him off duty and placed him on administrative leave until we're caught."

"Poor Jonah," she murmured. "I hope he doesn't resent helping us."

"Jonah is a good friend. He's angry, but not with us." Gage finished his food and balled up the wrappers. "He takes his oath to serve and protect very seriously. There were some problems with his uncle who used to be on the force, which is why he doesn't appreciate anyone attempting to tarnish his badge."

"Still, I feel bad he's put his career on the line for us."

Gage stared at her, then quirked a brow. "Sounds like you admire him."

She frowned at the slight edge in his tone. "I do admire him. It wasn't easy for me to trust the police, but I trust Jonah."

The muscles in Gage's jaw tightened. "Jonah goes to church regularly. He's very religious."

And Gage was telling her this—why? "I imagine a man who puts his life on the line every day has a good reason to have a close relationship with God."

"Maybe once this is over, you and Jonah can go out sometime."

"What? Are you crazy?" She couldn't believe he was trying to set her up with his friend. "I'm not interested in Jonah."

Gage avoided her gaze. "He's more your type than I am."

For several long moments she could only stare at him in shock. "Gage, what are you trying to say? I know I lost my memory, but I thought we were a couple. I wouldn't date another man if I'm already involved with you."

"What if you weren't involved with me?" he countered. "What if you broke up with me over a month ago? Would you be interested in Jonah then?"

"Broke up?" She could hardly comprehend what he was saying. "Are you really telling me we broke up?"

"I care about you, Alyssa. More than you could possibly know. I didn't lie about that. When we both thought you were Mallory, you assumed we were together, and I didn't correct you. But it's time you knew the truth." He paused, took a deep breath and met her gaze head-on. "You broke up with me, for the reasons I mentioned earlier."

She remembered he'd claimed she wasn't happy about the way he was so overprotective and that he didn't have a close enough relationship with God. Still, it didn't seem right that she would have broken up with him. Not when she was still so attracted to him. "I did?"

"Yes. You did." His mouth formed a grim line. "I don't blame you, but I want you to know, I have changed. I'm working on the overprotective part, and I've already learned the value of prayer."

His words thrilled her. "I'm happy for you, Gage."

"Thanks." He cleared his throat loudly. "I'm relieved to hear you're not interested in Jonah, because that means I can ask you to give me a second chance."

Gage held his breath, waiting for Alyssa's response. He'd tried to give her an out, knowing Jonah was far better suited for her than he was, but she declined and now he wasn't about to give her up. Not without a fight.

He ignored the tiny voice in his brain that warned him against getting too emotionally involved. When Alyssa's memory returned, she'd likely remember she didn't care about him in the same way anymore.

But he'd needed to lay his cards on the table, to make sure she understood how much he still cared.

"Gage, it wouldn't be fair for me to give you an answer now, when I still don't have my memory back."

His flicker of hope died. "I understand. And I didn't mean you had to give me a second chance right now, but once your memory has returned and we're safe, I hope you'll consider my request."

"Do you think my memory will return?" she asked with a troubled gaze. "What if it doesn't?"

"It will," he responded confidently. "The doctor seemed to think your memory will return, so we just have to think positive."

"Right." She gave a tight nod. "Think positive."

"Are you finished?" he asked. She'd finished her burger but still had half her fries left. When she nodded, he quickly took care of the mess. "We have to get ready to meet Jonah. Are you sure your ankle is up for another long walk?"

She grimaced but nodded. "I'll be fine."

He didn't believe her. "Have you been taking those meds the doctor prescribed?"

"Of course." She hesitated and then frowned. "Most of the time."

He wished she'd stay here, safe in the motel, but knew she wouldn't. He didn't push the issue. Hadn't he just claimed he was trying to change? Ignoring his screaming instincts, he waited for her to dig a dark sweatshirt out of their bag before opening the motel room door.

The sky wasn't nearly dark enough to suit him, although the dark clouds moving in helped a bit. At the fast-food restaurant several people were talking about the storm they were supposed to get later tonight. He hoped the rain would hold off until after their meeting with Jonah.

Rainbow Park wasn't that far, but he set a zigzag course, taking them well out of their way, just to be on the safe side.

Alyssa stumbled once and he quickly grabbed her arm before she could fall. "Lean on me," he offered.

She obliged him by putting her arm around his waist, allowing him to help support her. He knew her ankle must be causing her a lot of pain, and he swallowed a wave of frustrated helplessness.

Alyssa should be back at the motel, sleeping, with her injured ankle elevated on pillows, not being dragged through the dark city streets.

He slowed his pace to accommodate her needs. He didn't mind having her lean on him for support. In fact, he wished he had the right to hold her in his arms. Glancing at his watch, he realized he'd have to take the direct route from here if they were going to make the meeting on time.

"I'm slowing you down," Alyssa murmured.

"Don't worry, we're fine. We have almost fifteen minutes yet, and the park isn't that far from here."

She didn't say anything else as they made their way down one street and then took a left. He sensed her relax when she saw the sign for Rainbow Park.

The fountain was in the center of the park, and he swept a sharp gaze over their surroundings as they made their way along the well-lit path. He was glad the sun had gone down completely now. The darkness was their friend.

The fountain was up ahead and he slowed his pace, scanning the area for any sign of Jonah.

"Where is he?" Alyssa asked in a hushed whisper. "We're not early."

No, they weren't early. "I don't know," he admitted.

"Should we split up and search for him?"

"No, we're not splitting up." Not now, not ever as far as he was concerned. The park seemed deserted, but they couldn't afford to take chances. The back of his neck itched and his instincts were telling him that something was wrong. "Let's walk around to the other side," he instructed softly.

Could be that Jonah was hiding in the shadows until they arrived.

She tightened her grip on his waist and he tucked his cheek against her hair. He'd bought the red dye, but she hadn't taken the time to use it yet. He couldn't deny he'd miss her soft blond curls. Although he preferred her hair longer, the way it used to be.

The lights in the park were brighter than he remembered. Staying as close to the shadows as he could, he made his way off to a small patch of trees on the other side of the fountain. If Jonah was afraid he'd been followed, he wouldn't stand out underneath a streetlamp.

Once they reached the trees, he paused to give his eyes a chance to adjust to the complete darkness. "Jonah?" he whispered.

Nothing.

He took a few more steps and then stumbled against something soft. Was there something dark on the ground?

"Oh, no, Jonah?" He heard Alyssa's horrified gasp.

No. Not Jonah, too. Not after losing Dan. His heart pounded with dread as he dropped to his knees and felt for Jonah's wrist. A pulse. He wasn't dead. They weren't too late. His friend was still alive.

For a moment overwhelming relief washed over him. *Thank You, Lord! Thank You for sparing Jonah's life.*

"Call 911," he said tersely, handing Alyssa his cell phone and then ripping off his shirt to hold pressure over Jonah's bleeding abdominal wound. "Tell them to hurry!"

ELEVEN

Alyssa peered through the darkness, barely making out Jonah's ashen features. A wave of helplessness hit hard. When would this nightmare end? As soon as the thought formed, she was ashamed of herself. She needed to trust God's plan. Her fingers shook as she quickly dialed 911 on Gage's cell phone. After giving the dispatcher their location, she snapped the phone shut. She shoved aside a wave of hopelessness and knelt beside Gage. "Let me see how bad he's hurt."

"It's too dark to see much," Gage said, his voice terse. "I think he may have been stabbed in the side."

She kept her fingers on his pulse, reassured by the faint beat. "Is the weapon still in the wound?"

"No. But I'm assuming this is another knife wound, similar to Dan's, but lower and to the side, as if Jonah sensed his attacker behind him and turned at the last minute."

"Here, use this." She shrugged off her hoodie and handed it to him. "You'll need to use your body weight for pressure to stop the bleeding. If the knife wound nicked the liver he'll be in danger of losing lots of blood." As Gage followed her instructions, she ran her hands along Jonah's arms, legs and the rest of his body, blindly searching for other injuries. A large lump on the back of his head was the only additional injury she found.

"I feel like we're sitting ducks out here," Gage murmured. "I hope this isn't a trap."

She sucked in a harsh breath, glancing around fearfully. She sensed Gage moving and she quickly grabbed his arm. "Don't leave me."

"I won't," he assured her. "We need to move him closer to the streetlights," he said thoughtfully. "The police will come with the ambulance. Officer Crane could have done this himself, and is right now waiting for the call to come across his radio."

The mere thought of Officer Crane showing up made her pulse kick into triple digits. Once again, she glanced around, feeling as if there was a large bull's-eye painted on her back. "He'll arrest us for sure this time."

"We're not going to let that happen," Gage said grimly. The wail of sirens filled the air. "Come on, help me move him."

She gripped Jonah's legs, while Gage moved

up to his heavier upper torso. Together, they managed to shift Jonah closer to the fountain and the bright overhead streetlights. When Gage stepped back and reached for her hand, she shook her head. "No, we can't leave yet. Not until we find a rock or something heavy to place over his wound."

They both began searching even as the sounds of sirens grew louder, indicating they were close.

"Here's one." Gage lifted a large rock and put it on top of her hoodie. The sirens grew louder and she couldn't help glancing fearfully over her shoulder. "Let's go."

"I can't leave," she whispered. Leaving Jonah here, alone and injured, went against every fiber of her being. Even though she felt certain this was a trap set by Crane. Even if Crane wasn't the one who responded, there were likely warrants issued for their arrest. "Wait for me behind the trees," she urged.

"I'm not leaving you alone," he argued.

"You have to—we'll attract too much attention otherwise." She caught a glimpse of the red lights from the ambulance, and the police car wasn't far behind. "Hurry!"

Gage finally moved back into the shadows, just when the ambulance pulled up. Two men jumped out and grabbed their supplies out of the back before hurrying over.

"What do we have here?" the first paramedic asked, as he kneeled beside her.

"Deep penetrating flank wound on the right. May have nicked his spleen. He has a pulse, but I'm afraid he's been down for a few minutes."

"What happened?" the second paramedic asked as the first one quickly started a large-bore IV in Jonah's right arm.

"I—don't know. I was just walking through the park on my way home and found him like this." The police car pulled up, and she knew she had just seconds to leave. "Excuse me, I think I'm going to be sick."

She bolted away, lunging for the protection of the trees. Gage grasped her hand and she followed his lead as he melted into the darkness, moving quickly but quietly.

Lord, please keep Jonah safe in Your care, Amen.

Gage's heart was pounding so loudly, he feared the police could hear it. He should have insisted they leave before the paramedics arrived, but it was too late now. There were some trees providing coverage, but then there was a wide-open area they had to cross before they could seek shelter in the thicker grove of trees.

"Stay low and run toward those trees as fast as

you can," he said, his mouth close to her ear. "I'll be right behind you."

She didn't argue, and she managed to sprint faster than he'd given her credit for as she made her way toward the sanctuary of the trees. He stayed right behind her, protecting her in the only way he could, expecting to feel the hot streak of a bullet hitting him in the back.

Alyssa reached the trees and he followed two seconds later. He thought he may have heard a shout, but he didn't bother to look back. The trees offered protection as they weaved their way in a diagonal pattern toward the northeast side of the park.

"This way," he said, tugging on Alyssa's arm. She stumbled, and he reached out to grab her before she could fall. All this running had to be excruciating for her injured ankle. "Are you okay?"

"I'm fine." She obviously wasn't the type to wallow in self-pity.

He risked a quick glance behind them but didn't see anything other than trees. So far so good. Turning forward, he tried to envision where the road was. Following his instincts, he changed their direction slightly, and soon they found the road. There were houses on the other side, across from the park, and he led the way toward two that didn't have any lights on in the windows. Ducking between them, he ran through the backyards to the next street down, praying they didn't stumble across any dogs.

He could hear Alyssa's heavy breathing and tried to slow down, for her sake. But he kept cutting through people's backyards to confuse anyone who might be trying to follow them.

Fifteen minutes later, Alyssa slowed to a stop, bending over and putting her hands on her knees. "Break," she croaked. "I need to rest."

They weren't far enough from Rainbow Park to relax their guard, but he could see Alyssa was at the end of her strength. She'd kept up with him admirably. He glanced around, trying to get his bearings, wishing they were closer to the motel.

There used to be a small all-night diner just a couple of blocks away. "Can you manage just a little longer?" He anchored her arm around his waist, encouraging her to lean on him. "Two more blocks then you can rest for a bit."

She nodded wearily and he half carried her to the diner. It was a public place, but he didn't know what else to do or where to go. His only trusted police contact was right now on his way to the hospital, fighting for his life. Jonah couldn't help them anymore.

They were on their own.

Gage grit his teeth and held on to Alyssa as he

crossed the street and approached the diner. He could only pray no one inside would recognize them from the earlier newscast.

The place was surprisingly crowded and ancient tunes blared from an equally ancient jukebox. Gage was grateful for the crowd of people as he made his way to the back, where the restrooms were located. A few of the customers glanced at them curiously, but most ignored them.

"Oh, no," Alyssa whispered in a horrified tone.

"What's wrong?"

"We're covered in Jonah's blood." Her voice was brittle, as if she might collapse at any moment. In the dim light of the diner, he could see she was right. Both of their hands were streaked with blood and there were dark smears on their clothes, as well. Luckily, those stains were not as obvious, since they were both wearing dark colors to blend in with the night.

"Here's the bathroom. Do your best to wash up, okay?"

Alyssa stumbled into the ladies' room, closing the door behind her. He grasped the door frame for a moment, grappling with the need to keep her in sight at all times. Finally he turned to follow his own advice, washing off the evidence of Jonah's blood.

His buddy was a good cop. One of the best. The

only person he could imagine getting past Jonah was another cop. Crane? Or someone else? He wished he could be sure. Without Jonah's help and support, he felt as if they were stranded at sea in a canoe without paddles. What they needed was a plan.

Too bad his exhausted brain couldn't seem to come up with anything feasible.

Alyssa scrubbed her hands and arms until the pink-tinged water ran clear. She tried her best to soak the bloodstains from her clothes, without much success.

Bracing her weight on the porcelain sink, she closed her eyes. Fatigue oozed from every pore. Running on foot from the police was getting old. Yet the only person who'd believed their story was Jonah. Poor Jonah, who'd been stabbed because he'd tried to help them.

She sighed and tried to pull herself together. Jonah would be fine. He'd had a decent pulse and the paramedics had arrived quickly. He stood a very good chance of recovering. She'd have to call Trinity later to see if Diana was working in the ICU. Diana would let her know if he made it through surgery.

Abruptly she straightened and stared at her reflection in the chipped mirror. Diana? The image of a petite woman with delicate facial features and chin-length dark hair filled her mind. A memory?

She tried to remember more, but the blurred image wouldn't give any hint as to where she and Diana may have been. Likely the hospital, but her brain didn't even give her that much. Still, the surge of excitement was enough to banish her fatigue. Tiny flashes of memory were coming more and more frequently, usually when she least expected them.

Squaring her shoulders with renewed determination, Alyssa cupped her hands and splashed cold water on her face. Maybe she and Gage had suffered a setback tonight, but they weren't beaten yet.

Together, with God's help, they'd find a way to get through this.

She huddled next to Gage at a small table in the back of the diner, gratefully sipping a large, cold glass of water. "I remembered something," she said in a low tone.

Gage's eyes brightened eagerly. "You did? What?"

She felt bad for getting his hopes up. "Nothing that will help us, really, but as I was washing up in the restroom I thought about Jonah, and a colleague's face and name flashed in my mind. Diana White is a friend of mine who works in the ICU at Trinity."

"That's great, Alyssa," Gage said. "The fact that you're starting to remember is a good thing. Maybe if you can get one night of decent sleep, you'll remember more."

"Maybe," she acknowledged. They hadn't been given any time to rest since they'd discovered her true identity. "Anyway, I was thinking I could use your phone to call Trinity Medical Center, see if they have any news about Jonah."

Gage nodded thoughtfully. "You could, but it's still early. Only about thirty minutes since we ran from the park."

"They'd rush him to the hospital and he could already be in surgery by now." She leaned forward. "Gage, I really need to know if he's at least made it that far."

With obvious reluctance, he handed over his phone. She dialed the number and put her free hand over her ear to drown out the noise from the wailing jukebox. There was a loud beeping in her ear but then she heard ringing. When the operator answered, she requested to be put through to the trauma ICU.

"Trauma ICU, may I help you?"

"Is Diana White working tonight?"

"Yes, just a minute please." The elevator music returned for several long seconds, until a female voice came over the line. "This is Diana. May I help you?"

"Diana, this is Alyssa Roth."

"Alyssa?" Diana's voice rose dramatically. "Where are you? Did you know the cops where here looking for you? What's going on?"

The police had shown up at Trinity? Her stomach clenched at the news. The police had put the name Mallory Roth out as being a person of interest, but obviously they'd thought she'd give them information regarding her sister. "I don't have time to explain, but I need to know if you received a new patient, a cop by the name of Jonah Stewart?"

Diana gasped on the other end of the line. "How did you know? You didn't stab him, did you?"

"Of course not!" How could Diana even ask that question? Unless the police were spreading that rumor? The lump in her stomach congealed and sank. Soon, there wouldn't be anyplace left to hide. "He was hurt helping me. Is he all right?"

"He's in surgery. And you know hospital privacy rules prevent me from telling you any details. I can tell you he's in surgery because that's already been on the news and there are cops swarming the place. Alyssa, who stabbed him? What's going on? If you're in trouble—"

"Look, Diana, I don't know anything about who stabbed Jonah, and if you care about me at all, you won't tell the police I called. Goodbye." She snapped the phone shut before Diana could ask anything more. She handed the phone to Gage. "I heard something beeping in your phone. Is it low on batteries?"

"Could be." Gage took the phone. "I have some battery life yet, but there's a message. I don't remember the phone ringing."

She watched him punch in the code needed to listen to his voice mail. "Who is it?"

"Jonah. He must have left the message before he got hurt. He discovered there was a police response to your town house late Friday night, early Saturday morning."

She frowned. "Really? The same night I ended up in the emergency department? What time did you come and pick me up?"

"About three in the morning. They called me at two-thirty."

"Maybe I called the police, before I lost my memory?" She was trying to reason through the possible scenarios, but it wasn't easy without a memory.

"No, that's what Jonah found so odd. There wasn't a record of any calls to the dispatcher or to the 911 operator referring anyone to your address. In fact, there wasn't a record of the police response to your town house that night."

What? That didn't make any sense. "Then how does he know there was a police response?"

"He said he had a conversation with a rookie who mentioned a response that was abruptly called off. The rookie thought it was weird, especially when he was told not to record it."

"A cover-up," she whispered. A bloody room flashed in her mind. Was it possibly at her town house? Or somewhere else?

"Exactly." Gage scrubbed his hands over his face. "I'm sure they covered up some crime, but what, I don't know."

"Murder." The word popped out of her mouth with conviction. The bloody room had to be a memory fragment.

"Without a body?" Gage sighed and shook his head. "Although maybe there is a body. Maybe one in the morgue as a John or Jane Doe."

The thought of Mallory possibly being dead made goose bumps ripple across her skin. She didn't remember her twin sister, but she didn't want to lose her, either. "I doubt there would be a record of the body." At his puzzled expression, she continued, "Don't you see? If there's no paper trail recording the police response to my address, there can't be a body turning up at the morgue. You can't have one without the other."

"Are you ready to walk back to the motel?" he asked when Alyssa finished her water.

He thought she winced, but she gamely nodded and slid out of her seat. "As ready as I'll ever be."

They slipped outside, leaving the anonymity of the crowded diner. Immediately, he felt more conspicuous out on the road. The shrill ringing of his phone startled him. Apprehensively, he pulled it out, relieved to notice the call was from his dad.

Arizona was in a different time zone. His father was calling at eight at night, his time. "Hi, Dad," he greeted his father. "How are you?"

"Hugh Jefferson called me."

The blood drained to the soles of his feet. "What? When?"

"Just now. He said I needed to arrange a meeting for the three of us, and I had the impression that it wouldn't be healthy to refuse his request."

His dad's voice sounded far away, as if he were on the other end of a long tunnel. It took a moment to realize his hearing was obstructed by the high-pitched buzz of pure fury. How dare Jefferson use his father to get to him? His father was innocent—he had no part in Jefferson's sick game. This time, Jefferson had gone too far.

And then it hit him. Northwestern University. The place where his dad had gone to college all

those years ago. The same place Gage had gone.
The same place Hugh Jefferson had gone?

No wonder Jefferson had targeted Drummond
Builders. He'd purposefully used someone he
knew he could threaten and blackmail to do what
he wanted.

"You need to get out of there, Dad. Right now."
He clenched the phone so hard, his fingers hurt.
"Take Margaret on a trip. Use a rental car. Don't
tell anyone where you're going, not even me."

"What's going on, Gage?"

"I'm sorry, Dad. Jefferson is trying to use you to
get to me." Jefferson had found his Achilles' heel
and made no qualms about using it to his advantage.

There was a long silence. "Why?"

To make me finish his condos. As soon as the
thought formed in his mind, he knew it was true.
Jefferson knew that Gage would want to pull out
of the contract, and he was threatening his father's
life to get him to keep working for him. The bleak
realization weighed heavily on his shoulders. He'd
failed to protect his mother all those years ago,
when her second husband started beating her, but
this was worse. Much worse. He couldn't protect
both his father and Alyssa at the same time.

"I'm working on a project for him, but we're not
in agreement as to how things should be done."

The biggest understatement of the year. "Don't worry, I'll take care of things here. But I need you to be safe, Dad. I'm begging you to get out of there. Right now. Take a trip with Margaret."

"You think we're in danger."

"Yes. Leave the house and don't come back until you hear from me."

"Okay, then, we'll go. One of the advantages of early retirement is that we can pretty much do whatever we want. I'll take Margaret out of here, but I want you to keep in touch, Gage. I'm worried about you, too."

"Don't worry, I'll stay in touch. Take care, Dad." He paused, before adding, "I love you."

"Right back at you, son."

Gage closed his eyes and snapped his phone shut. He stared at the cell phone for a minute, fighting a wave of fury.

"Gage?" Alyssa gently touched his arm. "Are you all right?"

"No. Jefferson has dragged my father into this with an implied threat. Either I do what he wants or he'll hurt my father. I've asked him to leave town, but it's very possible Jefferson has criminals working for him in Arizona. I hope it's not too late." For a moment he was tempted to give in, to do whatever Jefferson wanted in order to protect the ones he loved. Never had he felt so helpless, not since he was ten years old and watching his mother suffer his stepfather's big meaty fist.

Ruthlessly, he shoved those memories aside. Failure wasn't an option. Somehow, he needed to figure out how to get out of this mess. Giving in to Jefferson's demands would be signing his own death warrant—once the project was complete, anyway.

No. Somehow, some way, he needed to keep Alyssa and his father safe.

TWELVE

Alyssa listened with horror to Gage's blunt assessment of Jefferson's latest stunt. Was there anything Hugh Jefferson couldn't do? Did he have people working for him everywhere? Gage was afraid his father wasn't safe, even all the way across the country in Arizona. And she understood why. What she didn't know was how to stop Jefferson's evil plan.

Please, Lord, help me remember!

"Is there anything I can do to help?" she asked when they'd walked a few blocks in silence.

"No." She didn't think she'd ever heard Gage sound so defeated.

Suddenly, his dejected tone made her mad. "Listen, Gage, we can do this. We're smart and resourceful. We've dodged Jefferson and Crane so far. And don't forget, we have God supporting and guiding us."

He glanced at her but didn't respond. She didn't

want to push, or preach, but surely he'd feel better if he shared his burden with God?

She could feel Gage tense when the headlights of a car approached, but they kept walking and soon the car passed them by. "How much farther until we reach the motel?" she asked, half dreading the answer.

"Not that far, especially if we take a few short-cuts."

Unfortunately, Gage's shortcuts meant sneaking through more backyards. A dog started barking loudly from the yard next to them, making Alyssa jump out of her skin. By the time they arrived back at the motel, she wanted nothing more than to shower and climb into bed.

As they approached the motel, she noticed a convenience store nearby. She glanced at Gage. "Do you have a couple of dollars? I want to buy another newspaper."

He glanced at her as if she were crazy. "Why?"

She shrugged. "So far, we learned a lot from the paper that was left on the bus, but it was Friday's paper. I thought a more recent newspaper might give us more information."

Gage nodded thoughtfully. "Can't hurt. Wait here, I'll get it."

She wanted to protest but honestly didn't have the energy. Times like this, she didn't mind Gage's protective attitude so much. If only he'd learn to strike a balance. She rested against the building, relieved they were nearly at the motel. Her ankle was throbbing like mad.

Gage returned quickly with the newspaper tucked under his arm. She sensed his nervousness as they hurried across the street.

"What's wrong?" she asked.

"Nothing, probably just my overactive imagination," he muttered.

Her gut clenched. More possible danger? Would she ever be able to relax again? "Tell me."

"It seemed like the clerk was staring at me," Gage admitted slowly. "I have a bad feeling he recognized me from the news."

Despite her physical exhaustion, Alyssa spent a restless night. Between the pain in her ankle and being afraid the police were going to come arrest them, she woke up every hour on the hour.

At seven, she gave up hope of getting more sleep. There was a tiny coffeepot on the dresser and she brewed a pot as she dyed her hair. Putting the red coloring over her blond curls wasn't easy, but she had to admit, the end result wasn't too bad. She certainly looked different.

Her blue eyes were still pretty distinctive, though, and the only way she could think to disguise them was to buy cheap clear glasses, since she didn't wear contacts and wasn't about to start now.

There was a brief knock at the connecting door between them and she glanced over to find Gage standing in the doorway. "Good morning. How did you sleep?"

"Terrible." Gage was staring at her red hair in shock. "I didn't think you'd actually use it."

She rolled her eyes. "You bought it for me to use, right? I don't have the option of growing a beard."

He scratched at his dark jaw with a grimace. "It itches."

She flashed a grin. "Don't look at me for sympathy."

"Okay, Red."

"That's the oldest nickname on the planet," she said with a groan. She liked this feeling of camaraderie that seemed to have sprung between them. Did their relationship before her memory loss have that same closeness? Somehow, she didn't think so, not if she broke up with him. She gestured to the tiny pot. "Want to share my coffee?"

"Yeah, and I bought breakfast." He set the bagels and cream cheese on the small table. "Figured with all the walking we've been doing, we could use a few extra carbs."

No argument there. She ripped a bagel in half

and spread a thin layer of cheese over it before taking a huge bite. She chewed thoughtfully for a moment. "We need a game plan."

"Did you read the newspaper?" he asked.

She shook her head. "Not yet."

"I skimmed it this morning, and there was a huge article about the special mayoral election being held tomorrow."

"Tomorrow?" She nearly choked on her bagel and then remembered Jonah had mentioned something about that the previous night, when they were at the first motel room. "I forgot it was Election Tuesday." Her memory hadn't suddenly returned when she woke up this morning, but even so, she sensed she wasn't big into politics. "Obviously Eric Holden is the main candidate, since he's the interim mayor, but who's the other candidate?"

"A Hispanic guy by the name of Gerald Maas. Interestingly he's a former city councilman himself." Gage took a deep sip of his coffee, capturing her gaze over the rim. "I figure anyone opposing Eric Holden is a friend of ours. My plan is to find Gerald Maas and see what, if anything, he knows about all this."

She had to admit, it was a good plan. They finished their breakfast and she found it difficult to tear her gaze from Gage's face. Even with the scruffy growth of his beard, he was very attractive. He'd asked for a second chance, and right now, she was willing to give him one. Would she feel differently when her memory returned? It was hard to imagine.

When they left the motel on foot, Alyssa wanted to weep at the pain that zinged up her leg. She ground her teeth together, determined to tough it out. Gage had enough to worry about without her adding to it by whining.

"Dan's truck!" he said abruptly, snapping his fingers. "Why didn't I think of that sooner?"

"Dan's truck?" Maybe it was lack of sleep combined with only one cup of coffee, but she wasn't following him. "What about Dan's truck?"

"I have a key." Gage dug into his jeans pocket and pulled out his wallet. "I'm sure Dan's truck is parked down by our offices."

Since Gage's office building was on the other side of town, she didn't consider this revelation particularly good news. "It will take all day to walk there," she protested. "We have to figure out some way to find Gerald Maas."

Gage sent her a sidelong glance. "And you think I don't have faith?" he asked dryly. "The newspaper listed his campaign headquarters, and since the election is tomorrow, I'm sure someone will be there, maybe even Gerald himself."

She blushed and realized he was right. She was

tired, crabby and in pain, but that was no excuse to lose faith. "Brilliant idea, Gage. Although I'm almost afraid to ask where the campaign office is located."

"Not to worry. We can take the number ten bus downtown, pick up Dan's truck and then go to the campaign office. Piece of cake."

Gage's good mood was contagious. She admired him for putting his fear for his father aside, at least on the surface. She found herself thinking she was very lucky to have Gage at her side during all this. She couldn't imagine what she'd have done without him.

Cautiously, they made their way past the convenience store without incident. "Guess the clerk didn't recognize you after all," she murmured.

"I hope not, but regardless, once we have Dan's truck, I think we'll come back here, get our stuff and find a new place to stay for the night." Gage's expression turned grim. "No sense in pushing our luck."

She had to agree. They found the bus stop and had to wait only a few minutes for the bus to arrive. With her red hair and Gage's darkly shadowed jaw, she didn't think they'd look too much like the photos on the news. But she kept her head down and avoided direct eye contact with other passengers as she slid into a seat in the back of the bus.

The ride downtown took longer than she expected, as the bus stopped many times along the way. But once they reached the end of the line, she was grateful they weren't far from the parking garage. "Where do you think he parked?" she asked.

"He has a white truck. There, it's the third one from the end."

The thought of actually driving from point A to point B was enough to pick up her mood. She'd never been so happy to see a vehicle in her life. Gage slid behind the wheel and started up the truck with a twist of the key.

Riding to Gerald Maas's campaign headquarters took less than ten minutes to cover a distance that would have taken at least an hour or more to walk.

Inside, the place was busy with people picking up fliers for one last campaign push. "Can I help you?" a harried, rather buxom woman with blond-streaked hair asked when she saw them standing there.

She noticed Gage put on his most charming smile. "Good morning, ma'am. We're both huge supporters of Gerald Maas. Would you happen to know where he is?"

"Supporters?" her brown eyes gleamed. "How would you like to canvass some neighborhoods for us?"

"We'd love to!" Alyssa blinked when Gage readily took a handful of Maas for Mayor fliers. "But we really need to talk to Gerald, first. Is he swinging by here soon?"

"No. If I know Gerald he's down on the river, fixing up that old railroad property of his."

"Railroad property?" she echoed, glancing over at Gage. He shrugged, indicating he had no idea what the woman meant.

"You know where the old Milwaukee railroad used to cross the river?" When Gage shook his head no, she went on, "Right across the street from the south end of the Summerfest grounds. The old brick building used to be the control tower for the railroad bridge. It's not in use now, of course, but the building is still there. Would make a nice little place for a restaurant or deli. Any property on the water is worth something these days."

Yeah, like Jefferson's condos overlooking the river. "Oh, yes, of course," Gage said. "I know exactly where it is. Thanks so much."

Back out in the truck, she glanced at him. "How did you know where she was talking about?" she asked.

"Because I know the downtown area pretty

well." He pulled out into traffic, and once again she was thrilled not to be walking. "It's actually not far from here."

Five minutes later he pulled off and parked the white truck. As they approached, she noticed the two-story narrow brick building with large windows on three of the four sides overlooking the Milwaukee River. It was cute, too small for condos, but as the woman mentioned, perfect for a small restaurant or deli.

"There he is," Gage murmured.

She followed his gaze. There was a small concrete patio in the back of the control tower building, overlooking the water. Two plastic chairs were back there, and a middle-aged man, with black hair liberally sprinkled with gray, sat pensively looking out over the water.

As they closed the distance, he spoke without turning around. "Nice day for fishing isn't it?"

"Uh, yes sir." Gage took the lead, coming up to stand beside the former councilman. "My name is Gage Drummond and this is Alyssa Roth. We'd like to ask you a few questions, if you don't mind."

Gerald narrowed his gaze suspiciously. "You reporters?"

"No!" she exclaimed. "We're not Eric Holden fans, and we're concerned about what will happen to the city if he wins this election."

The older man looked between them and then nodded slowly. "All right, then, please sit down." He indicated the plastic chair next to him.

She glanced at Gage, silently asking where they should start. He cleared his throat and turned toward the former councilman. "Mr. Maas, we know that Hugh Jefferson is financially supporting Eric Holden's election, and that greatly concerns us. We have reason to believe Jefferson is dangerous."

Maas slowly nodded. "Councilman Schaefer said the same thing to me about a couple of weeks ago. And now he's dead."

She sucked in a harsh breath. "Why?"

Maas lifted one shoulder. "Schaefer took the lead in voting against giving him a permit. But in the end, the rest of the group was swayed in favor of granting the permit because of the additional tax revenue, ignoring Jefferson's shady business deals. And you're right, Holden will likely win this election. I'm trying my best, but I don't have the clout that Jefferson has."

"We need to stop him," she urged, leaning forward. "Help us stop him."

Maas lifted tired brown eyes to hers. "Unfortunately, there isn't much I can do. No one is listening to me. If you have any sort of proof regarding Jefferson, you should take it directly to the police."

"We can't," she protested softly. "He has officers, at least one for sure that we know of, working for him."

"If we had concrete proof, we could take it to the FBI," Gage offered. "Do you know anything that can help us?"

Maas was silent for a moment. "I have my suspicions of course, just like others do. But I couldn't find any proof to support my theory."

She frowned and exchanged a look with Gage. "What theory?"

"That the previous mayor, Tony Flynn, was murdered."

Flynn murdered? Stunned, Gage stared at Maas. "I thought the autopsy proved he died of a heart attack?"

Maas's tone was bitter. "Pretty convenient heart attack, if you ask me. I don't believe it. Flynn was disgustingly healthy, ran marathons on a regular basis. He didn't have a family history of heart trouble. And he was found crumpled over his desk after a late meeting with Holden."

"Anyone can have sudden death from a heart attack," Alyssa protested. "Even a marathon runner."

Maas waved a finger at her. "I know what you're saying, missy, but I still don't believe it. Mayor Flynn wasn't one to fold under pressure. Are you really going to sit there and tell me that there isn't something that can be given to a person that mimics a heart attack, even on autopsy?"

"The only thing I know of is potassium chloride," she whispered, looking stricken. "An injection of potassium chloride would mimic a heart attack, and the higher levels of potassium in the bloodstream would be associated with the actual event itself."

Gage was shocked. "But it can't be easy to get your hands on potassium chloride," he protested.

"Not easy," Alyssa acknowledged. "Every hospital in the country keeps the stuff secured in the pharmacy. No vials are allowed up on the nursing units. But still, nothing is impossible."

Maas grimaced. "So now you know why I can't help you with proof. They're too good at covering their tracks."

Gage hated to admit failure, but after asking a few more questions, he realized Maas couldn't help them any further. "Thanks for your time, sir. And I hope you win this election."

"I hope so, too." Gerald Maas set down his fishing pole to stand and shake their hands. "Good luck."

"Thanks." He cupped Alyssa's elbow in his hand, offering her support as they made their way back to Dan's truck. He could tell by the way she was walking that her ankle still bothered her. He wished he had thought about Dan's truck sooner.

"So now what?" she asked when they reached the truck. "Maas didn't help much, except to reinforce our suspicions."

"I know, but somehow it makes me feel better to know we have at least one ally." Gage drummed his fingers on the edge of the steering wheel. "Let's run back to the motel, pick up our stuff and find a new place to stay for tonight."

"Sounds good." She sat back against the seat with a sigh. "Thanks, Gage."

He lifted his eyebrows in surprise. "For what?"

A small smile tugged the corner of her mouth. "For being here with me through all this. I'm so glad to have your support."

He was humbled by her words. He didn't deserve her gratitude—he still felt responsible for her current state. Still, she was right in that they had a lot to be thankful for. "You're welcome, but you need to know, the feeling is mutual."

She reached over and put her hand on his. He clasped her small hand in his, wishing he had the right to pull her into his arms and kiss her. He tried to keep his concentration on the road, but he was all too aware of Alyssa beside him.

"Um, Gage?" The underlying fear in her voice

cut through his thoughts. "There's a squad car behind us."

He glanced up at the rearview mirror, and his gut tightened with fear. Almost instantly, the red and blue lights went on, and the squad car came up right behind them, practically touching their rear bumper, indicating they needed to pull over. "Can you tell if the driver is Crane?"

"I don't know. I can't see past the sun glare." She twisted in her seat and then glanced at him. "There's too much traffic. We'll never be able to lose him."

"We'll get arrested if we pull over." He swept a frantic glance over the area. To the right there was a road, relatively free of cars, that wound beneath the interstate. "Hang on," he said as he yanked the steering wheel, making a sharp right.

Unfortunately, the police car followed, red and blue lights still flashing.

"Gage!" Alyssa shouted. "Look out, he has a gun!"

Desperately, he swerved again, but too late. The bullet hit its mark and their rear tire blew, sending the truck sliding out of control. He wrestled with the steering wheel, slamming on the brakes to try to avoid the concrete pillar. He managed to slow the vehicle down, but the front end of the truck still smashed into the pillar with enough force to cause the air bags to deploy.

Instantly, he was pinned in his seat, listening to the shattering glass of the windshield.

"Gage?" The air bags began to deflate, and he felt Alyssa's hand gripping his arm. "Are you all right?"

"Yeah, but we have to get out of here." He shoved his door open, but a strong hand stopped the door from opening all the way. The ruddy face of Officer Crane loomed before him, a cruel smile twisting his thin lips. The gun he'd used to shoot out their tire was leveled at Gage's chest.

"Well, well, well. This must be my lucky day." The deep, mocking drawl made him clench his fingers on the steering wheel in anger. Especially when Crane leaned over to leer at Alyssa. "Did you really think the red hair would fool me?" he asked snidely. "Get out. You're both under arrest for the murder of Dan Kirkland."

Gage wanted nothing more than to wipe the satisfied smirk off Crane's face, but the gun held him immobile. They were trapped. There was no way out of this one. He didn't doubt that Crane would shoot them both if they tried to run. He couldn't bear to look at Alyssa as he slid out of the driver's seat. He couldn't face how he'd failed her yet again.

"Up against the car, both of you. Hands behind your back."

Cage stood helplessly against the truck, and Alyssa soon joined him. Crane snapped plastic ties around his wrists, locking them together. From the corner of his eye, he watched Crane place the same type of plastic ties around Alyssa's wrists.

"This way." Crane kept the gun in one hand, using it to urge them both to the back of his squad car. He opened the back door and waved the gun, gesturing for them to get in. Gage waited for Alyssa to scoot in first, then slid in beside her. Crane slammed the door behind them.

Crane slid into the driver's seat, picked up the radio and began speaking. "Dispatch, I'm reporting an abandoned vehicle, a white Chevy pickup, license 555 ERP, registered to a Daniel J. Kirkland, deceased. It's located under the Marquette interchange. No sign of the driver or any passengers at this time. Send a tow truck to the scene, over."

"Ten-four," the radio squawked.

Crane replaced his radio, started the car and then eased into traffic. Dread curled in Gage's gut. "You're not taking us to the police station, are you?" he asked.

Crane let out a mirthless laugh. "Ooh, you're so smart, Drummond. No, we're not going to the police station."

Beside him, he heard Alyssa's sharp gasp.

Defiantly, he met Crane's gaze through the rearview mirror, refusing to show the man any trace of fear. Crane's eyes were bright with triumph. "Jefferson has other plans for the two of you." His evil gaze shifted to include Alyssa. "I can hardly wait for both of you to get what you deserve."

THIRTEEN

Red dots of fury swam before Gage's eyes. He strained against the ties binding his wrists, ignoring the increasing pain in his arms. He had to protect Alyssa. To keep Crane from laying one slimy finger on her.

His fault. Once again, this mess was his fault. Why on earth had he picked up Dan's truck? His stupidity had gotten them captured. For a moment, a wave of helplessness washed over him.

Lord, please help us! Guide us and give us strength to escape Crane!

The silent prayer helped to steady his racing heart.

"Where are you taking us?" Alyssa's voice held a fine tremor, although the stubborn tilt to her chin was reassuring. Her show of bravery made him even more determined to find a way to escape Crane.

"Anxious to be alone with me, babe?" Crane

taunted. The way his leering gaze lingered on Alyssa caused Gage to grit his teeth in frustration. "Maybe we can have a little fun together after I get rid of your boyfriend."

Gage kept his expression impassive, refusing to let Crane know how much his taunts were getting to him. He forced the red haze of fury away and he stared out the window, making mental notes of which streets Crane took. The only advantage they had at this point was that Crane hadn't checked their pockets prior to slapping the plastic cuff ties around their wrists. Gage carried a small Boy Scout knife in the front pocket of his jeans, a gift from his father many years ago. With his hands behind his back, the knife wouldn't be easy to reach, but at least they weren't completely helpless.

He refused to believe there wouldn't be a chance to escape. Alyssa told him he needed to put his faith in God, so he would. *Help me, Lord. Help me find a way out!*

Crane headed west, the opposite direction than Gage had expected. Crane turned on National Avenue and then turned right again, heading under the 35th Street viaduct to a section of the city that once housed many manufacturing plants. Now only old, dilapidated warehouses remained. With a sinking feeling, Gage quickly realized the area looked deserted.

The police car slowed to a stop in front of an old warehouse at the end of a dead-end street. Crane pulled a keyring out of his uniform pocket and unlocked the heavy padlock on the door. After raising the garage door, he got back in the squad car and pulled the vehicle inside the warehouse. Crane closed the garage door with a loud bang.

Darkness enveloped them. After a minute, Gage's eyes adjusted to the dim light. There were windows high on the walls of the warehouse, practically covered in grime. His heart sank as he realized the windows were a good ten feet off the ground. The rest of the warehouse was mostly empty, except for a few crates and boxes lining one wall, many appearing to be rotted or broken.

Crane abruptly opened the door closest to Alyssa. "Hey, babe," he greeted her, as if she happened to be voluntarily spending time with him instead of being kidnapped. Crane grasped Alyssa's arm and pulled her out of the squad car, still holding the gun in his right hand. Gage edged across the seat to scramble out after her, as if his presence alone might keep her safe. "You're a real looker, aren't you?" Crane said, using the barrel of the gun to trace a line from her neck down toward the open collar of her shirt.

Alyssa held her head high, as if she wasn't afraid of being mauled or worse, although fear and loathing shone from her blue eyes.

"You think you have your bases covered?" Gage asked sharply, desperate to divert Crane's attention from Alyssa. "We just talked to Gerald Maas. He knows you murdered Flynn, Schaefer and Dan Kirkland. Don't you think the body count is a bit steep? I mean, really, how many deaths can you blame on gang members?"

Crane swung his head around to scowl at Gage, although his gun hand never wavered. Then he widened his eyes with feigned innocence. "Me? I didn't kill anyone. You're the one who murdered Kirkland. And we have plenty of evidence to prove it."

"Like what?" Gage needed to keep him talking, both to keep him from getting too close to Alyssa and to know exactly what they were dealing with.

Crane stepped closer to Alyssa, the tip of his gun brushing her skin, and she automatically took a step backward. One step, two steps, three. Gage subtly eased along with them, trying not to let Crane get between him and Alyssa.

"Your fingerprints on the knife in his chest. Documents that show Kirkland stole money from Drummond Builders to pay off gambling debts,"

Crane bragged. "Let's see, I believe that's both motive and opportunity."

"Fabricated evidence," Gage summarized bitterly. Dan hadn't been a gambler, although he didn't doubt Crane's ability to plant anything he wanted to support his false claim.

"Enough evidence for the D.A. to file charges." Crane abruptly laughed. "If you refuse to cooperate with us, that is. We have to keep you alive long enough to finish the condo project."

Alyssa was still moving backward, away from Crane's gun, when her heel caught on the stack of crates behind her. She stumbled and fell backward against the wooden crates.

Just when Gage feared the worst, that Crane would actually attack Alyssa right before his eyes, the radio blared from inside the squad. "Unit 19, are you there? Unit 19 come in, please."

For a moment, Gage wondered if Crane would ignore the summons. The ruddy-faced cop was staring intently at Alyssa as if he'd never been this close to a woman before. Finally, after what seemed like an eternity, he gestured toward Gage with the gun. "Get over there next to her."

Gage gladly complied, coming over to crouch next to where Alyssa was still sprawled against the crates. With her arms bound behind her back and her bum ankle, she struggled to get back on her feet.

"Don't move," Crane warned as he backed up to the squad car. He opened the front passenger door and reached across for the radio. "Unit 19 responding, over."

"Unit 19, the chief wants you to report to his office, pronto."

The chief? As in the chief of police? Gage couldn't tell if Crane was upset by this new directive or not. Was it possible the chief of police was on to Crane? Or was he also a party to Jefferson's illegal activities?

"Ten-four, I'll be there in fifteen." Crane put the radio back, his teeth gleaming in a feral grin. "Duty calls, but don't worry, I'll be back shortly."

Gage estimated they were a good twenty feet from the garage door. Maybe when Crane opened it to get the squad car out, could they run through the opening?

Almost as soon as the thought formed in his mind, Crane came toward them. "Get to the farthest corner of the warehouse and sit down on the floor. Now."

Since Crane still held the gun on them, they had little choice but to obey his curt command. Alyssa managed to use one of the crates for leverage to get back on her feet. Gage stayed right beside her as they walked to the farthest corner of the warehouse.

"Jefferson wants you alive, but if you try to run, I'll be forced to shoot you in the leg," Crane told them in a flat, emotionless tone. "I earned expert status in marksmanship, so don't doubt my ability to hit what I'm aiming at. Understand?"

Gage nodded, understanding only too well as he slid down the wall next to Alyssa. Right now, he was willing to wait for Crane to leave before trying anything further. He sat as close to Alyssa as possible, his arm pressed against hers in an attempt to give her strength and support.

Crane backed up to the garage door, opened it up and then returned to back the squad car out. He left the car idling while he shut the door with a definite thud.

Alyssa closed her eyes in relief when Crane left. The man's lewd stare made her feel sick to her stomach. She knew he'd intended to touch her, or worse.

Thank You, Lord, for sparing me.

"Alyssa, get back up on your feet," Gage hissed in an urgent whisper, cutting into her silent prayer. "We don't have a lot of time."

Her ankle was throbbing worse than before, from

tripping and falling against the crates, but she resolutely inched up the wall behind them.

"Can you reach into my front pocket?" Gage asked, positioning himself behind her.

She felt for the edge of his front pocket with her fingers, but Crane had put her wrists together so tightly, there wasn't much room to maneuver. "I can feel the top edge of your pocket," she confirmed.

"Scoot down and try to slide your fingers in. See if you can get hold of the pocketknife," he directed.

Gage had a pocketknife? For the first time since she saw the cop car behind them, she believed they might actually have a chance to escape Crane. She crouched down a bit and worked her fingers into the front pocket of Gage's jeans. She could feel the smooth plastic of the pocketknife, but grasping it and pulling it up seemed nearly impossible.

"Take your time," Gage murmured encouragingly.

The plastic ties cut sharply into her wrists, but after several failed attempts, she finally managed to get the knife gripped between her first and second fingers. Drawing it carefully upward, she finally pulled the small pocketknife free and folded it into her palm. "Got it," she cried.

"Great! Now hand it to me." Gage turned around so they were back-to-back, enabling her to pass the knife. Opening the knife wasn't too difficult, and he finally ran his thumb across the sharp edge of the blade.

He tried to maneuver the sharp edge against his own plastic ties, but he couldn't get enough leverage. After several tries, and several cuts to his hands and wrists, he gave up. "Alyssa, you need to take the knife handle and use the blade to cut through the plastic."

"I can't see what I'm doing. What if I hurt you?" she asked. "Maybe you should cut through mine instead."

"No!" his abrupt refusal startled her. "Don't worry about cutting me. You can do this, Alyssa. We need our hands free in order to find a way out of here."

Alyssa bit her lip and took the smooth handle of the knife in her fingertips. "Okay, I have the knife. But I can't tell where the tip of the blade is."

"Leave that part to me," he assured her. "Just make sure you don't lose your grip on the knife, okay?"

Easier said than done, as the plastic coating felt slippery from sweat. She held the knife as firmly as possible as Gage moved closer. There was pressure on the other end of the knife, and she heard Gage suck in a harsh breath. Had she cut him? "Are you all right?"

"Fine," he said through gritted teeth. She could feel him pushing against the knife as he worked to get it into position. Something warm and slippery trickled over her fingertips, and she knew he must be bleeding. "There, the blade is right under the plastic cuff. I'm going to push my wrists down while you keep the pressure with the knife steady, okay?"

"Okay." She did as he asked, and after a few attempts the plastic tie broke free.

Gage dropped his arms to his sides and then turned to take the knife from her fingers. "Hold still," he murmured as he used the knife to cut through the plastic ties binding her wrists. "You're free."

"Oh Gage!" she spun around and threw herself into his arms. He clasped her close, crushing her tight. She buried her face against his chest. "I was so scared," she confessed in a muffled tone.

"Shh, I know. It's okay." She could feel his cheek resting against her hair.

She wanted to stay in Gage's arms forever, but obviously, getting their wrists free from the plastic ties was only the first step in escaping. They were still locked in the warehouse. With effort, she pulled away and glanced around. "Do you think we can get through those windows up there?"

"We're going to try," Gage said grimly. He

crossed over to the pile of broken crates and gingerly picked up one and set it on the other.

Bright red blood dripped from his fingertips. "Gage, you're bleeding. Did I cut you?"

"Just a nick, I'm sure." He ignored his injury and continued to pile one crate on top of another under the window with the least amount of grime.

"Wait a minute," she demanded when blood continued to flow down his wrist. "That cut is way too deep. I need to put a pressure dressing over it."

Reluctantly, he paused long enough for her to take the elastic bandage from his earlier injury and apply it to his wrist instead. The cut in his wrist looked far too deep for comfort. But there wasn't much she could do without first-aid supplies, so she wrapped it up as tightly as she dared before joining him in piling the crates on top of each other.

"We have to hurry. Crane could come back here at any moment." Gage tested his weight on the crates, causing them to shake and groan.

"I should go up. I'm lighter," she pointed out.

"I'm taller." Since she couldn't argue that, she did her best to hold the wobbly crates still as Gage climbed up to reach the window. "It's stuck shut. Hand me a piece of wood. I'll break it open."

She did as he asked, ducking her head when pieces of glass fell to the floor around them. Gage took his time, making sure there were no shards of glass left in the frame. He was high enough that he could easily lever himself out of the window, and she had to bite her tongue to stop from begging him not to leave her here alone.

"Stand back, I'm coming down."

"What? Why?" Despite her initial fear, she knew that Gage needed to get out of the window to bring help of some kind.

He shot her an exasperated glance. "You're going through first."

She shook her head as he dropped down beside her. "I don't know if I can do it, Gage."

"Sure you can. I'm not leaving you in here alone. You have to shimmy through the window. It's large enough that you should be able to pull yourself up, swing your leg through and then drop over the other side."

She stared at the rectangle-shaped window dubiously. "I don't know, Gage. Maybe you should go and get help."

"Leaving you here isn't an option, Alyssa." His determination and support was heartwarming. "Either you go or neither of us gets out of here."

She let out a heavy sigh and then cautiously began climbing up the pile of crates. They didn't shake as much under her weight, and she reached the top in no time. She grasped the bottom of the window frame and tried to pull herself upward, but she didn't have enough arm strength.

"I'm coming," Gage said. The tower of crates swayed dangerously and she clung to the window frame, holding her breath, praying the rickety crates would hold their combined weight. "Okay, I've got you." With Gage pushing her up from below, she was able to get her torso through the window and balance on the edge long enough to get her leg up and over. From there, it wasn't nearly as hard to get her other leg over the window frame. She hung there for a moment, wishing she knew how far the drop would be, and soon decided it didn't matter. One way or another, she was going down.

Give me strength, Lord, she prayed and then let go. Her feet hit the ground hard and a sharp, stabbing pain shot through her ankle as she fell backward on her bottom. She managed just barely to keep her head from hitting the ground, too.

She looked up and saw Gage was already making his way through the broken window. She scooted out of the way just in time for him to land on the ground beside her.

"Alyssa? Are you all right?" He knelt at her side.

"I need help to get up," she told him. He gave her a hand and she kept all her weight on her good leg as he slowly pulled her upright. "I don't know if I can walk," she confided, fighting tears of frustration.

"Lean on me," Gage encouraged.

She did as he asked, but even with his support, she couldn't put any weight on her ankle. "I can't do it, Gage. I can't walk." Close. They were so close to escaping. Panic clawed up her throat, choking her. "Gage, how are we going to get out of here?"

Gage could tell Alyssa was close to losing it. He battled a wave of dizziness as he glanced around, looking for something for her to use as a cane. The elastic bandage she'd wrapped around his wrist was already bright with blood, and the way the wound wouldn't stop bleeding, he suspected she'd hit an artery when she'd cut away the plastic cuffs.

"Here, see if you can use this for support." He picked up a hunk of pipe that happened to be lying on the side of the warehouse. If she could manage to walk with the pipe, he hoped they could get out of sight.

Yet it wouldn't be easy to hide in broad daylight, especially now that they were both injured. He refused to give up hope, though. They'd gotten this far, hadn't they? God had already given them the strength to escape the warehouse. Surely they could lose themselves in the anonymity of the city.

He was proud of the way Alyssa grasped the waist-high length of pipe and leaned on it as if it was a cane. Deep lines of pain bracketed her mouth, but she took a few wobbly steps and then glanced at him. "This will work for a while, so let's go."

Gage glanced around, trying to pick the best escape route. Too bad there weren't a lot of options. "We'll have to avoid the main road, since we know Crane is heading back this way. Let's go behind the warehouses and see where that takes us."

Alyssa nodded gamely but didn't say much as she slowly moved beside him, leaning heavily on her makeshift cane. As they rounded a third warehouse, they came across an old, rusted bicycle with tires that were low on air but not completely flat.

"Can you get up on the seat?" he asked, holding the frame steady.

"Yes, but how are we both going to fit?" she asked skeptically.

"I'm going to stand and pedal while you hang on to my waist." Pedaling on low-pressure tires took a lot of strength and effort, but he refused to give up. At least not until they managed to get somewhere safe.

Riding double was awkward, but he made decent time, especially when they could coast downhill for a few blocks. Each yard he was able to put between them and their warehouse prison made it easier to breathe.

Gage tried to think of a place to go, but he didn't know of any other motels that would take cash without asking too many questions. Not to mention the stream of blood oozing down his arm.

Alyssa must have noticed too, because she tightened her grip around his waist. "Gage, we need to find some first-aid supplies." She was balancing precariously on the seat, with her legs outstretched so they wouldn't interfere with his pedaling. "You're losing too much blood."

He didn't answer, because he knew she was right. If he didn't find a place to rest and get off the bike soon, he might very well fall off. And where was he supposed to find first-aid supplies? Their duffel bags were probably still in the back of Dan's truck, which meant he had only the money in his wallet and nothing more.

Wait a minute—Alyssa had a first-aid kit in her town house. As a nurse, she'd prided herself on having the best first-aid supplies. He'd avoided her town house until now, because he'd considered it too dangerous to go back.

But their options were severely limited by their

respective injuries. They wouldn't stay overnight, but they could at least pick up the first-aid kit, and maybe a change of clothing. And best of all, her town house was only a few miles away.

With a firm destination in mind, he pushed himself to pedal harder and faster. Cautiously, he first rode past the town house, making sure there was no one staked out there, before heading around the block.

"Where are we?" Alyssa asked hesitantly as he pulled up in front of the cheery white building.

He'd almost forgotten her amnesia. "At your town house," he murmured, rolling the bike to a stop. He put his foot down on the ground and then held the bike steady for Alyssa. "I have a key."

"You do?" She looked horrified by the thought.

"Don't worry—I promise I didn't stay here with you, Alyssa. You only asked me to keep it as a spare. You gave a key to your sister, too." He bypassed the front door, preferring to use the less conspicuous side door. He quickly unlocked it, pushed the door open and then held out his arm so that Alyssa could lean on him to hobble inside.

She took several steps, looking around curiously. He was relieved the place looked the same way as it did a few days ago, when he'd come here to look for Alyssa the morning after he'd picked her up from the hospital. He'd left the windows open, so the pine scent wasn't as overwhelming as it had been before.

Alyssa leaned against the wall, favoring her sore ankle as she worked her way down the hall to the bedrooms. Were the surroundings familiar to her at all? Curious to see her reaction, he followed close behind. When she reached the master bedroom, she froze.

"What is it?" he asked, putting his arm around her. Her shoulders were shaking, and he knew she was crying. She stayed there for so long, he began to get worried. "Alyssa? You're scaring me. What's wrong?"

"I remember," she finally whispered in a low, agonized tone. "Gage, I remember!"

FOURTEEN

In a rush, memories tumbled through her mind, falling into place like dominoes. Councilman Schaefer bleeding on a stretcher, telling her Jefferson's thug stabbed him. Officer Crane refusing to believe her, and then later trying to run her off the road. Hiding in a flea-ridden motel and borrowing her twin sister's identity. Searching for Mallory. A glittery hair clip on the living room table. Blood pooled on her bedroom floor. A bloodstained yellow blouse crumpled in the corner.

Mallory!

She gripped her stomach as pain sliced deep. Her fault. Her twin had been killed because someone had mistaken Mallory for her! Guilt rolled over her, beating her down like tidal waves, threatening to send her crashing to the floor. Slowly, she sank to her knees, covering her face with her hands. *Lord, help me. Please, help me. If Mallory is dead, please bring her home to You.*

"Alyssa? What is it? What do you remember?"

Gage's deeply concerned voice and his strong hand on her shoulder finally penetrated her inner turmoil. She remembered how he'd proposed marriage while on a horse-and-carriage ride. And she remembered breaking off their engagement, because he'd suffocated her with his protectiveness and he hadn't embraced his faith. But she still cared about him. More than she'd admitted before. With an effort, she tried to pull herself together.

"Mallory," she whispered in a hoarse voice. "I remember my twin. She died because of me."

She heard Gage suck in a deep breath. "She died? You actually found Mallory's body?" His tone was incredulous as he glanced around as if trying to picture what she'd seen.

"No." She could barely get the word past a throat tight with grief. "I found her hair clip on the table in the living room, so I knew Mallory had been here. When I walked into my bedroom, there was blood and a stained yellow blouse over there. In that corner." She gestured with her right hand. "There was so much blood—I can't see how she could have survived. Don't you see? I was in danger—Crane followed me and tried to run me off the road. Mallory came here, and they must have killed her by mistake!"

Gage's grip on her shoulder tightened. "I'm not

surprised that Crane tried to kill you. But, Alyssa, you don't know for sure that Mallory is dead. Isn't it possible the blood wasn't hers? Maybe she fought off her attacker and somehow managed to escape?"

She stared at him in shock. She'd been so certain Mallory was dead, but maybe, just maybe, Gage was right. Was it possible Mallory had escaped a horrible attack? Fragile hope bloomed in her heart. With all the blood, she'd honestly expected to find a dead body, but she hadn't. She wanted very badly to believe Gage was right. "But if Mallory is still alive, where is she? Why wouldn't she call me or try to find me? Why wasn't she at home in her condo?"

"I'm not sure," Gage allowed. "But remember, you haven't been home for a while. I stopped by here a few days ago, and the pine cleaner scent was overpowering. I knew something was wrong because you always use vinegar to clean. Now I believe Crane or Jefferson had this place cleaned to hide the scene of a crime. That's why the pine cleaner scent was so overpowering. Maybe they deleted a message from Mallory. Or maybe Mallory thought for some reason she was the one in danger, and that by leaving she'd protect you from harm."

Alyssa knew the latter was a very strong possibility. Her twin was extremely protective, to the point of doing outrageous things, like flirting with Gage to make sure he truly cared for Alyssa. If Mallory for some reason thought she herself was the target, then absolutely, Mallory would take off to protect her.

She lost her cell phone, which was another reason Mallory couldn't have gotten in touch with her, even if she'd wanted to. "If only I hadn't lost my cell phone, there might be a message from Mallory on there," she murmured, remembering her mad dash through her neighbors' backyards as she'd run for her life. Until she'd fallen, rolling down the hill. "We have to find her, Gage. If there's any chance Mallory is alive, we have to find her."

"We will," he assured her. "Once we're safe, we'll look for your sister until we find her."

Alyssa felt something warm dripping on her arm, and her gaze settled on the blood-soaked bandage around his wrist. "I'd almost forgotten why we came here. That cut is really deep—your wrist shouldn't still be bleeding like that."

He grimaced. "I know. I think the artery might be nicked."

She scrambled to her feet, ignoring the shaft of pain that shot up from her ankle. "An artery?" she echoed, appalled with herself. What kind of nurse was she? Knowing that Gage needed immediate medical attention made it easier to push her grief and worry for Mallory aside. "Sit down in the kitchen and hold pressure while I get the first-aid kit from the bathroom." She remembered exactly where she'd stored her first-aid kit and was relieved the infernal fog was lifted from her mind.

Thank You, Lord, for the return of my memory. And please, keep Mallory safe in Your care.

She grabbed the first-aid kit from the bathroom closet and hobbled into the kitchen. Gage was sitting on the table, holding pressure on his injured wrist. He looked pale, and she suspected he'd already lost too much blood. She opened the kit, took out her supplies and then went over to the kitchen sink to get soap, water and towels.

She gently cleaned his wrist. The gash in his skin was much larger and deeper than she'd realized. Her guilt must have shone on her face, because he quickly spoke up. "Not your fault," he said firmly. "You couldn't see what you were doing, and neither could I. We were lucky to escape with only minor injuries, so don't make this worse than it is. I'm sure a pressure dressing will work just fine."

"I don't think so," she murmured, not at all happy with the way blood constantly oozed out of the cut. "This is too deep. The artery needs to be stitched closed. We need to get you to a doctor."

"No hospital, no doctor," he curtly refused.

"You're a nurse, Alyssa. If it needs a suture, do it yourself."

She stared at him in horror. He didn't understand what he was asking. "If the arterial blood flow to your hand is damaged, you could lose circulation to your fingers," she argued. With two fingers, she pressed hard on the area just above the open cut and the blood flow stopped. She held it for a full minute, hoping the collateral circulation would work. She tested his fingers, making sure they stayed pink and warm.

"We don't have a choice, Alyssa," he told her. "You're strong and I know you have the skill and ability to do this. But you have to hurry—we aren't safe here for long. I'm sure once Crane discovers we've escaped from the warehouse, he'll think to check here at some point."

He was right. As much as she hated the thought of hurting Gage, or possibly causing irreversible damage to the circulation in his hand, they didn't have time to waste. His wrist needed immediate care. "Okay, hold pressure right here." She indicated the area she wanted him to press. "I'll need to find a needle and thread."

Gage nodded and did as she asked. She stood and bit back a cry of pain when her sore ankle took her weight. After she took care of Gage's wound, she planned on wrapping her ankle with an Ace bandage.

She found her sewing kit without problem and took it back into the kitchen. She gathered her small scissors, gauze, tape and antibiotic ointment. She found a small box of matches in her kitchen junk drawer and lit one to sterilize the needle.

After she had everything she needed, she returned to the kitchen table. "Are you ready?" she asked, feeling sick to her stomach. She hadn't sutured anyone up while they were wide-awake and able to feel what she was doing. "This is going to hurt."

"I know. Just do what you need to do."

She wished she didn't have to do anything, but his calm acceptance helped steady her. She carefully examined the wound. The area she needed to stitch wasn't on the surface, but down inside the cut. His arm jerked when she gently inserted the needle. "I'm sorry," she murmured, blinking the tears from her eyes so she could see what she needed to do. Caring for strangers in the emergency department was far easier than sticking Gage with a needle. She felt every flinch as deeply as if she were poking a needle into her own skin. "I'm sorry," she repeated, helplessly.

Sweat beaded on her forehead and rolled down the side of her temple as she concentrated on the task at hand. Six long, agonizing stitches later, she dropped the needle with relief. "There. I'm finished." She washed the remaining blood away, and then liberally spread a layer of antibiotic ointment over her rather-uneven stitches before wrapping gauze loosely around his wrist. She felt dizzy, as if she'd been the one stitched up. She was amazed that Gage had been able to take the pain so well.

"Thanks, Alyssa," he murmured, his lips forming a faint smile. He lifted his uninjured hand to cup her face, his thumb lightly tracing the curve of her cheek. "I probably don't tell you often enough, but I think you're amazing."

Her breath caught, tangled in her throat. She gazed into his cinnamon-colored eyes and remembered how much she'd admired him when they'd first met. Gage had accompanied a crew member who'd gotten hurt on one of his construction sites. His caring and compassion for his employee, despite the accident being mostly the man's own fault for not wearing the proper safety gear, had immediately drawn her to him. He'd asked her out, and uncharacteristically, she'd agreed.

They'd gotten engaged within a few months. Too quickly, she realized now. Returning his ring and walking away was the hardest thing she'd ever done. But she couldn't marry a man who didn't celebrate his faith. And deep down, she knew Gage had just been going through the motions because she'd asked him to. Not because he wanted to.

"Alyssa," he whispered her name, drawing her close. "I know you're remembering all the reasons you left me, but please give me another chance to show you how much I've changed. I finally understand what you wanted for me, so don't write me off as hopeless. Please?"

She leaned into his embrace, wanting to do as he asked. Certainly, he wasn't hopeless. She managed to nod, mere moments before his mouth captured hers in a poignant kiss.

His mouth was sweet, gentle, yet insistent as it captured hers, sweeping away any lingering doubts. She reveled in his embrace, wishing she could stay in his arms forever.

Gage buried his face in Alyssa's hair, drawing deep breaths to steady his racing heart. He couldn't regret kissing her, even though he knew they needed to leave. Now. He fully expected Crane to show up at any moment. Reluctantly, he pulled away and forced a smile. "Let's find some clean clothes and then get out of here."

Alyssa sank into a kitchen chair. "I have to wrap my ankle, or there's no way I'll be able to walk even with a cane."

"Let me," he said, and quickly dropped to his

knees. When he saw her darkly bruised and swollen ankle, he felt awful. How could he ask her to walk? A surge of helplessness gripped him by the throat. She'd been so worried about the cut on his wrist, yet her ankle was just as bad, if not worse. It had to be broken. For sure, they'd have to continue using the bike. Gently, he took the Ace bandage and wrapped her ankle, providing some support, although not nearly enough in his opinion.

She loosened the laces on her running shoe and then slid it back on her foot. "Gage, I left my car in a park-and-ride not too far from here. That night, when I found the blood, I'd taken a bus, because I was worried Crane would try to follow me."

"You did?" He'd been dreading the return of her memory, knowing she'd remember why she'd left him, but now he realized her memory could be a tremendous help. "That's perfect. We can borrow your bike from the garage, and with both of us biking, we'll make decent time to the park-and-ride."

"Okay." Relief relaxed her facial features.

It took several precious moments to find and change into clean clothes, but he knew they couldn't easily rent a motel room wearing blood-stained apparel. Thankfully, Alyssa had a backpack and they stored some essentials, mainly granola bars and medical supplies for his wrist, and then they were once again ready to go.

Alyssa was pedaling slowly, as if even that much pressure on her ankle hurt. He was tempted to force her to ride double again, but he knew they'd look far more conspicuous if he did that.

The park-and-ride wasn't far, but it took them the better part of a half hour to get there. His heart sank when he didn't see her familiar car.

Alyssa scowled. "Where is it? Gage, I know I left my car right here," she gestured to the now-empty parking space.

"Let's look around, maybe with everything that's happened, you're not remembering it clearly."

But even though he circled the entire park-and-ride twice on his bike, he knew she was right. She'd no doubt left her car there, but it was gone now.

"Crane," she muttered under her breath. "I bet that lowlife probably had it towed, because he knew there was evidence of the crash on the driver's side, where he tried to sideswipe me off the road."

Gage nodded grimly. "I'm sure you're right. But let's look on the bright side—we have four wheels between us." His attempt at humor fell flat.

The shrill ring of his phone nearly sent him crashing off his bike. Hoping, praying it was his father, he quickly checked the number and saw it was Jonah's. But Jonah was in the hospital. "Hello?" he answered cautiously. Was this another trap? Had Crane gotten hold of Jonah's cell phone?"

"Gage? Where are you?" Although it was weak, he clearly recognized Jonah's voice.

"Jonah? How are you? Is everything okay?"

"I'm out of the hospital, but don't dare go back home." Jonah's voice was faint, and Gage had to strain to hear him. "I think we need to stick together."

He was all in favor of sticking together, but was Jonah stable enough to leave the hospital? He'd been stabbed just last night. He tightened his grip on the phone. "We're at the park-and-ride by Watertown Plank Road, and we can certainly meet you. I can't believe your doctor discharged you from the hospital."

"The doctor didn't discharge me, I left against medical advice. But only because someone tried to sneak into my room to finish off the job they started at the park. I'm better off taking my chances out here with you than being a sitting duck in my hospital room."

He reeled from the news. "We'd pick you up, but we don't have a car," Gage said to Jonah. Was it possible Crane or Jefferson had a nurse working for them? A nurse who'd sneaked into Jonah's room to try to finish him off? The same nurse who'd gotten hold of potassium chloride to kill Mayor Flynn?

"My buddy loaned me a car. I'll meet you along Underwood Creek Parkway in five minutes. I'm driving a black Ford Taurus."

"Alyssa and I are on bicycles and we'll head over that way right now." He snapped his cell phone shut. "We're meeting Jonah at the parkway."

"He shouldn't have left the hospital," Alyssa murmured as she turned her bike toward the north end of the park-and-ride. "He just had surgery yesterday."

"He claims someone tried to sneak into his room to finish him off," he said, relaying Jonah's story. "Claims his odds are better out here than stuck in his room."

"Maybe," she said, her tone betraying her doubt. "If he doesn't pass out from pain or infection. Good thing we packed the first-aid supplies. We're the three injured musketeers," she joked weakly.

He flashed a reassuring grin. "Yes, and we're just as resilient," he agreed.

The smile she flashed over her shoulder gave him hope that they might find a way out of this mess yet. Within a few minutes, they reached the parkway. This early in the evening, in the warm summer air, there were a lot of cars parked and many people running or riding bikes. They fit right in.

He spied a black car parked at the side of the road, isolated from most of the others. When they approached, the headlights flashed twice. "That's Jonah," Gage said in relief as he closed the distance, with Alyssa following close behind.

Jonah rolled down his driver's-side window as they approached. "You'll need to leave your bikes here. There isn't enough room for them in this dinky car. Hide them in the trees over there," he said, indicating the small patch of trees.

"Okay, but unlock the door, Alyssa needs to sit down. I'll ditch the bikes."

"Fine," Jonah said, unlocking the doors. "But hurry, I'm starting to get light-headed. One of you is going to have to drive."

Gage tossed both bikes in the deep thicket along the edge of the creek, and then hurried back over to the car. He wasn't at all reassured to find Jonah slumped over the steering wheel.

"His pulse is faint but steady," Alyssa said from the passenger seat beside him. Her worried gaze met his. "But you need to get us someplace safe soon, because Jonah needs fluids, antibiotics and rest—stat."

FIFTEEN

Alyssa kept her fingers on Jonah's pulse the entire ride to the motel. Thanks to a car with a full tank of gas, Gage was able to take them outside the city limits, off the main highway.

She was worried about Jonah. He'd obviously left the hospital too early. She could probably give him enough fluids and force him to rest, but antibiotics? They couldn't get a prescription for antibiotics without a doctor's order.

Gage pulled up to the motel and glanced at her in the rearview mirror. "I know you're tired and your ankle hurts, but it would be best if you could go in to rent the room. The red hair might throw them off."

His plan made sense, and with their limited reserves, she knew they couldn't afford two rooms anyway. She slid out of the car and took the money he handed her. Her ankle screamed in pain, but she resolutely ignored it and forced herself to walk into the motel lobby.

"I need a room for the night," she said, flashing the heavyset older man standing behind the counter a bright smile. "I hope you'll take cash, though, since I had to cut up my credit cards." She leaned forward and lowered her voice, as if sharing a dark secret. "I was addicted to QVC."

The old man smiled as she'd hoped he would and handed over an actual, old-fashioned key. "Sixty-two per night is the cash rate, Ms. er—?" He looked at her expectantly.

"Anderson, but please call me Amy." Sixty-two sounded like a lot, but she handed over the money and snatched the key off the counter. "Thanks so much."

"You're in room seven, at the end of the row. And checkout time is eleven o'clock," he added as she turned away from the counter. She gave him a tiny wave to show she heard him and left the lobby, leaning heavily against the wall to rest her ankle as soon as she was out of his line of vision.

The distance back to the Ford Taurus where Gage and Jonah waited seemed like ten miles instead of ten yards. Gathering every bit of strength she possessed, she pushed away from the wall to head back toward the vehicle, but she halted when she noticed the vending machine. She fed two dollars into the machine and pressed the button for a bottle of Gatorade. The stuff didn't taste very good in her opinion, but the electrolytes and sugar would help Jonah's dehydration faster than plain water.

"We're in room seven. Just give me a minute to unlock the door," she said to Gage through the open driver's window.

"I'll get Jonah. You rest your ankle."

As much as she wanted to do that, she didn't think Gage would be able to get Jonah's muscular frame inside without help. But she needn't have worried, because Gage and Jonah staggered in while she was still searching for something heavy to prop the door open. She was relieved to see Jonah was awake and walking somewhat on his own.

"Thanks," Jonah grunted when Gage helped lower him to the edge of the closest bed.

"I need to check your wound," she said, moving to his side.

"It's not that bad," Jonah protested wearily. "After surgery they told me I was lucky because my ribs deflected the tip of the knife away from my diaphragm."

She agreed with the doctor's assessment. A paralyzed diaphragm took away a person's ability to breathe on his or her own. "Did you lose the lower lobe of your lung?" she asked as she looked at his dressing. Thankfully, there was no sign of bleeding.

"Yeah. How did you know?" Jonah asked.

"Alyssa is a trauma nurse, remember?" Gage spoke up. "And that means you need to listen to her advice."

"Yes, starting with drinking this entire bottle of Gatorade," she informed him. "Honestly, Jonah, you shouldn't have left the hospital. Without antibiotics, your wound is likely to get infected."

"I have the bottle of antibiotics they gave me," he offered, pulling them out of his pocket. "And they were talking about sending me home in a day or two anyway, so what's the difference?"

She eagerly scooped up the bottle of antibiotics. *Thank You, Lord!* With God's help, she knew they could get Jonah back on his feet very soon. "Here, you're due for a dose now, and you can wash it down with the Gatorade."

Jonah did as she asked. "Gage, I know where to find Hugh Jefferson," he said, after he finished off the entire bottle of Gatorade.

"Where?" Gage demanded.

"I did some searching and discovered he has a boat slip down at the marina. The name of his private yacht is *Lucky Lady.*"

Food, hydration and rest worked wonders for Jonah. Alyssa was relieved and reassured when after twenty-four hours, he claimed he felt one hundred percent better.

"We need to plan our next steps," Gage said over

breakfast from a local fast-food restaurant. He'd slept on the floor without complaint. "We can't just keep hiding out at motels. We have an ally in Gerald Maas, but I'm not sure how much weight his opinion will carry, since he didn't win the election last night."

Eric Holden's landslide victory had been all over the news. She couldn't help feeling guilty that they hadn't been able to do more to help the best man win.

"I think we need to go down to the marina, to stake out Jefferson's yacht," Jonah murmured. "Maybe we'll catch something incriminating with my camera phone."

"I doubt he'll be so careless," she felt compelled to point out.

"He's arrogant enough to think he's above the law," Gage countered. "I agree with Jonah. He and I should head down to the marina. It's the only clue we have."

She froze, staring at Gage in shock. "You and Jonah?" she slowly repeated. "What about me?"

Gage avoided her gaze. "You should stay here and rest that ankle. We'll be back soon enough."

She couldn't believe that he was so willing to leave her here. What about being partners? What about being in this together? "I can't stay here. Checkout time is eleven o'clock. I'm going with you."

"No, you're not." Gage slapped some more money on the small table. "You're going to ask to stay another night, and then you're going to wait here for us, where you'll be safe." The sharp edge to his tone ripped her heart.

So much for his claim that he'd changed. Maybe he'd made strides with his faith, but he still refused to treat her as an equal partner. "Gage, I'll be safer with you and Jonah than staying here alone."

"No, that's where you're wrong, Alyssa." Gage rose to his feet, and this time, when he finally met her gaze, she could see he'd already made up his mind. "I've done nothing but drag you into danger, over and over again. You're staying here, end of discussion."

"End of discussion?" she echoed in horror. Gage was showing his true nature, and she wasn't sure she liked it at all. How dare he talk to her like this? Especially after everything they'd been through.

"Yes. And don't bother arguing. There's nothing you can say or do to make me change my mind."

Gage almost caved at the stark, wounded expression in Alyssa's blue eyes. But he knew how awful her ankle looked—rest was what she needed more than anything. Besides, what was wrong with keeping her safe? Being safe wasn't a bad thing, it was a good thing. He'd failed her when Crane had captured them, and it was only through a little luck and a lot of faith that they managed to escape. He couldn't stand the thought of failing her again.

"Don't do this, Gage," she implored him. "You told me you changed, that we were partners. I thought you trusted me. Trusted the Lord to watch over us."

"I do, but logically, there's no reason to put you in danger, Alyssa. We're going on a fact-finding mission, nothing more."

Jonah rose to his feet and edged toward the door. "I'll wait in the car while you two fight this one out," he murmured.

"There's nothing to fight about." He tore his gaze away from Alyssa's and followed Jonah to the door. "We'll be back before you know it," he shot over his shoulder before closing the motel room door behind him.

"Whew," Jonah whistled under his breath as they walked across the asphalt parking lot. "She's not happy with you, man."

Gage shrugged, knowing Jonah's words were a gross understatement. For a moment he hesitated, but then steeled his resolve and opened the driver's-side door to slide behind the wheel. "I'd rather she was safe and mad than in danger."

"I know what you mean," Jonah admitted. "But she was right about having faith, Gage. I don't think I'd be here today if not for God's love and support."

He glanced at his friend in surprise. He knew

Jonah was religious, but his buddy had never said anything like this before. "Really?"

Jonah nodded. "I accepted Christ years ago when my partner took a bullet meant for me. I almost quit the force, but it was only through church and renewing my faith that I was able to return to my job."

Gage remembered when Jonah's partner had died, but he didn't realize how traumatized his friend had been at the time. Now he felt guilty for his ignorance. "I'm sorry, Jonah. I didn't know."

His buddy shrugged. "I knew you were busy trying to keep your business afloat."

Yes, he had been, but his business shouldn't have been put ahead of his best friend. As he drove, he realized Alyssa had felt the same way, when he'd used work as an excuse not to attend her Bible study group. His business had claimed a lot of his attention, and that wasn't necessarily a bad thing. Except when it got in the way of his relationships. "I'm sorry, Jonah," he repeated. "I'm sorry I wasn't there for you."

Jonah raised a brow. "I'm not the one you should be apologizing to," he pointed out. "Alyssa is the one you just left behind."

"Only to keep her safe," he added. "You're injured. It's not as if we're going to take any chances here. For all we know, Jefferson's yacht isn't even in port." He glanced at the dashboard clock. "We'll be back at the motel in a couple of hours."

Alyssa made her way back to the motel office, with Gage's money clutched in her hand. She wasted fifteen minutes crying, grieving for something she'd never have, before she'd pulled herself together.

First she needed to secure the room for a second night. Then she needed to find some way to contribute to the investigation. She'd already used the phone book in the room to find Gerald Maas's phone number. Maybe the former mayoral candidate wouldn't mind coming out to the motel to pick her up.

The older man from yesterday wasn't behind the counter. A younger woman who might have been his daughter glanced at her curiously when she walked in. "May I help you, miss?"

Alyssa's smile was strained. "Yes, I'd like to keep the room for another night." She set the cash on the counter and pushed it toward the clerk.

The younger woman frowned a bit when she saw the money, and then her sharp gaze returned to Alyssa's face. For a moment, she wondered if the young woman recognized her. She resisted the urge to fluff her red hair as she returned the clerk's gaze. "Oh, you're the Amy Anderson in room seven, aren't you?" she asked. "My dad mentioned you didn't have a credit card."

Tension eased from her shoulders. "Yes, that's correct. Being addicted to QVC didn't help my credit rating, let me tell you. But I'm slowly paying off my debt, month by month."

"Hmm. I see." The young woman slowly took the money, counting the cash. "What brings you to the area?" she idly asked.

Alyssa tried to think of a plausible explanation. "Oh, I'm just passing through," she said vaguely, slowly backing away from the counter. "Thanks again for letting me stay," she said as she pushed through the door.

She could feel the young woman's gaze burning into her back, and she tried to walk normally down the sidewalk to her room. Her heart pounded in her chest and sweat gathered along the back of her neck. Probably just her overactive imagination, thinking the clerk may have recognized her from the news. Hadn't Gage thought the same thing the night before? And they'd been safe, hadn't they?

Inside her motel room, she used the phone to call Gerald Maas, but when there was no answer, she was forced to leave a message. Now what? The minutes seemed to pass by with excruciating slowness.

She stretched out on the bed and closed her eyes to pray. *Dear Lord, please keep Jonah and Gage*

*safe in Your care. And please grant us the strength
and wisdom to find the evidence we need to put
Jefferson and Crane behind bars. Amen.*

A sense of peace settled over her and she must
have dozed a bit, because her mind was still groggy
when she heard a sharp rap at her door. "House-
keeping!"

She swung her legs off the bed and crossed
over to the door. Remembering her earlier paranoia about the clerk recognizing her, she took a
minute to peer through the peephole. She could see
a small, gray-haired woman standing there alongside her cleaning cart. Relieved, she opened the
door. "I don't need anything except a few extra
towels," she began, only to stop abruptly when
Crane jumped out from behind the cart.

"No!" she cried, trying to slam the door in his
face. But he was too quick, and he slapped a hand
on the door, shoving it so hard she stumbled back.

"Well, well, well," he drawled, his evil grin leering at her from above. Horrified, she struggled to
get back on her feet. "If it isn't Ms. Roth, once
again."

"Help me," she cried out to the maid, but the
woman shook her head and backed away, taking
her cart with her. She was trapped. The only way
out was through the door where Crane stood.

"No one is going to help you," Officer Crane
said, reaching down to drag her roughly to her feet.

She could feel his hot breath against her cheek, and she struggled not to scream. "Where's your boy-friend?"

She shook her head, unwilling to say anything about Gage. When he ruthlessly snapped metal cuffs around her wrists, she couldn't do anything but pray.

Help me, Lord! Save me from this horrible, evil man and protect Gage and Jonah.

"Not talking, huh? Oh, you will soon enough, once Jefferson gets hold of you." His evil grin made her feel sick to her stomach. He dragged her toward his squad car. Out of the corner of her eye she could see the maid huddled against the wall. "Ms. Roth, you're officially under arrest for the murder of Dan Kirkland."

Gage had to park a few blocks from the marina, and as he and Jonah walked he told himself it was a good thing he'd left Alyssa behind, since walking would have been difficult for her.

But then again, he knew she'd walked much farther distances without complaining.

Had he made the wrong decision to leave her behind? He hadn't thought so, but now he wasn't so sure.

"Okay, we're looking for slip number thirty-one," Jonah said in a low tone. "And keep your eyes peeled for someplace to sit and watch without attracting attention."

He nodded and carefully looked at each boat as they approached the marina. The place was busy even midmorning on a Wednesday, although he saw many smaller boats, not bigger yachts like the one registered to Hugh Jefferson.

"Look over there." Jonah nudged him and gestured to the right. "See those bigger boats? I think one of those must belong to Jefferson."

Gage saw the area he meant. "Yeah, I see them. I can't read the names on the boats, though."

"We have to get closer." Jonah led the way along the pier as if he came down to the marina often. "There it is," he said excitedly. "The one on the end, see it? *Lucky Lady.*"

"I see it." Gage was intimidated by the sheer size of the boat. Had to be a good eighty feet long. "And there's a small sailboat on this side that's almost directly across from it. I think we should sit in that boat and keep watch."

"Okay," Jonah agreed. "But you'd better pray the owner isn't going to come down anytime soon."

"Don't worry, I will pray." Gage had never talked about prayer and faith like this with anyone except Alyssa before. But knowing that Jonah believed somehow made it easier to be open and honest with his friend.

As soon as they returned to the motel, he vowed

to make amends with Alyssa. And the next time they went out on a fact-finding mission, he was going to bring her along. Truthfully, leaving her behind hadn't helped his concentration any. In fact, his thoughts were torn between wondering how she was doing and the job at hand.

He and Jonah slipped into the sailboat and hunkered down so they were partially hidden by the mast. From their angle, they could see clearly into the back of the boat.

"No sign of Jefferson," Jonah murmured beside him. "But with a yacht that big, he could easily be down below in the cabin."

Gage made himself comfortable on a boat cushion, sensing they were going to be here for a long time. Although it occurred to him that if Jefferson wanted to escape on the boat, there wasn't anything they could do to stop him. They didn't even have a boat to use in pursuit. "The Coast Guard," he said suddenly.

Jonah glanced at him with admiration. "You're right, Gage, we should have thought of that earlier. The Coasties have the right to board any boat they want, for any reason."

That was an interesting fact Gage hadn't known. "I don't suppose you know anyone enlisted in the guard?" he asked.

"Actually, I do," Jonah responded slowly. "A guy by the name of Rafe DeSilva. He's stationed up at

Sturgeon Bay, but they make their way all around the Great Lakes."

"Try calling him," Gage urged. "If he doesn't answer, then leave a message."

Jonah looked uncertain. "Gage, what am I going to tell him? That we suspect Jefferson is a crook and they should board his boat? What if they don't find anything?"

Gage let out his breath in a heavy sigh. "I guess you have a point," he murmured. "We should wait until we have a good reason to call."

Suddenly, Jonah gripped his arm, hard. "I think we have our reason, Gage. Look! Isn't that Crane walking down the pier with Alyssa?"

Gage's heart leaped into this throat when he saw Crane walking alongside Alyssa, heading directly toward Jefferson's yacht. Her wrists were free, but he could tell by the way Crane held her close to his side that the dirty cop had a gun pressed against her. "Call the Coast Guard, now," he urged Jonah. "Before it's too late!"

Jonah already had his phone out to make the call. Gage watched helplessly as Crane urged Alyssa onto the boat. He shouldn't have left her alone. And he wouldn't leave her alone now. Without saying anything to Jonah, he stood, rocking the small sailboat, and dove into the water.

Jefferson's yacht wasn't leaving without him.

SIXTEEN

"Step into the boat," Crane growled into her ear. Shaking with fear, she did as he commanded. The moment she was on board the engine rumbled to life beneath her feet. Crane kept the gun aimed at her as he quickly unmoored the boat from the slip and then jumped on board. Within seconds the boat slowly drifted away from the pier.

"Welcome aboard the *Lucky Lady,* my dear," a gravelly male voice said from behind her. "It's a beautiful day for a boat ride, wouldn't you agree?"

Alyssa slowly turned to face Hugh Jefferson. He was dressed impeccably in a white shirt and white slacks, as if they were truly headed out for a simple pleasure cruise. He flicked a piece of lint from his sleeve and then gestured to the inner cabin behind him. "Ladies first."

She swept a quick glance around, frantically hoping to catch some onlooker's gaze, but no one seemed to pay them the least bit of attention as the boat slowly backed away from the pier. The sun was out and seagulls swooped and dived over the water, searching for food. The scent of fish was strong, making her feel sick. For a moment she was tempted to dash forward and throw herself in the water, but she held herself back.

She needed to have faith in God. Not to mention, faith in both Gage and Jonah. Surely they were close by and would sound the alarm. Who was piloting the boat? She didn't know and was afraid to ask. Reluctantly, she moved forward, brushing past Jefferson as she went down the short hall to the private sitting area of the yacht.

He followed right behind, too close, as she could feel his hot breath on the back of her neck. "I've been waiting for this moment for a long time, *Alyssa,*" he hissed.

The sound of her name instead of Mallory's caused her heart to drop like a stone. Jefferson knew her real identity? She walked forward, across a plush carpet lining a ridiculously extravagant sitting room. Stubbornly, she lifted her chin. "Really, Hugh, I'm appalled you've mistaken me for my twin sister," she bluffed.

"Alyssa, you underestimate me," Jefferson drawled. He pushed her in the small of her back, making her stumble forward, pain zinging up her injured ankle. She grasped the edge of what looked to be a well-stocked bar and then slowly turned to face him, her stomach twisting with dread. "Did you really think your poor dye job and pathetic attempt to evade me actually worked? I've always known your true identity." His gaze narrowed dangerously. "Now, if you want to live, you'll tell me where to find both your sister, Mallory, and your boyfriend, Gage Drummond."

Hearing his name caused Gage to flatten himself along the side of the luxurious yacht, his heart pounding so loud he could barely concentrate. Slowly, he inched along the wall, edging as close as he dared. Hopefully, Jonah would soon send the Coast Guard after them, because now that he was on board, he wasn't sure what he could do to help.

He just knew he couldn't leave Alyssa to face Hugh Jefferson and Creepy Crane alone.

"Would you like something to drink, my dear?" Jefferson asked as if he were entertaining guests. "I'm sure you must be parched. I have an excellent selection of wines or single-malt Scotch, if you prefer something smooth."

"No, thank you," Alyssa responded politely.

Gage could hear the distinct sound of ice clinking against glass, and he assumed Jefferson was pouring himself a drink. "Have a seat," Jefferson encouraged. "You won't be getting off this boat anytime soon, so you may as well get comfortable."

"If you knew who I was all along, why attack Mallory?" she boldly asked. "Why not keep coming after me?"

"Yes, I must admit, your sister's escape was not part of the plan," Jefferson said, his voice taking a hard edge. "In fact, I was most displeased with the man who failed me. He deserved to die."

Gage swallowed a lump of fear. Jefferson obviously didn't care how many lives he took, as long as he got what he wanted.

"You should have let me take care of her, boss," Crane said in a bragging tone. "She wouldn't have gotten away from me."

"You?" Jefferson's voice was dangerously soft. "Have you forgotten how you let Alyssa escape not just once, after your pathetic attempt to run her off the road, but a second time, when you had both of them locked in the warehouse?"

Another long pause. Gage couldn't help a sense of satisfaction at how easily Jefferson knocked Crane down a few pegs.

"Wasn't my fault I was summoned by the chief because he wanted an update for his press conference," Crane argued hotly. "You need me, Jefferson, and don't forget it."

"You think so?" Jefferson said softly. "I wouldn't be so sure."

Gage held his breath, hoping the two men would keep fighting. He continued to edge along the side of the boat, scanning the water for any sign of the Coast Guard.

There was another long silence, and Gage went still. Had he inadvertently done something to attract attention?

"Now what?" Alyssa demanded loudly, so loudly she was nearly shouting. What in the world was she doing? "Are you going to kill me? Toss me overboard? What?"

She was trying to warn him. Gage started to back up, but seconds too late. Crane stepped around the edge of the boat, his gun pointing straight at Gage's chest. Belatedly, he realized the water dripping off him had made a small trickle that had rolled down, alerting Jefferson and Crane to his presence.

"Good timing, Drummond," Crane said, flashing his evil smile. He waved the gun, motioning Gage forward. "You're just in time to join the party."

Alyssa was horrified when Gage entered the room, followed closely by Crane holding the gun. The moment she'd noticed the steady stream of water, she'd suspected Gage was on board, but unfortunately, being trained as a police officer, Crane had noticed it, too.

The creep had been desperate to get back into Jefferson's good graces. Capturing Gage on Jefferson's boat hadn't hurt.

"Let's kill them both now," Crane said, his gaze darting nervously between Alyssa and Gage. If she didn't know better, she'd think the cop was actually intimidated by Gage. "We can dump their bodies overboard and they'll be fish bait before they're ever found."

"Excuse me, who put you in charge?" Jefferson asked softly. The softer his tone, the more nervous Crane appeared. Jefferson turned toward Gage, inclining his head regally. "Drummond, so glad you could join us."

"Stop it!" Crane shouted, his hand starting to shake. "We have them both, and Holden won the election by a mile. What do we need them for? You can find some other builder to use as a front for your money laundering. We need to shut them up, permanently!"

"For once, I agree with Aaron," a third voice said. Alyssa couldn't believe it when Eric Holden stepped into the room. She glanced at Gage, a mirroring dismay clearly reflected in his eyes. She knew exactly what he was thinking. Their odds were dwindling fast. How many others did Jefferson have stashed on his massive yacht?

"Holden, I told you to stay below." Jefferson's face turned red. Alyssa edged closer to Gage, seeking reassurance.

"I don't follow your orders," Holden snapped. "I'm the one with the power now, remember? Without me, you'll never get additional building permits. Besides, our boss is the one who calls the shots, not you."

Jefferson seemed to wrestle his temper under control, staring at Holden with frank disdain. "We'll do this my way," Jefferson reminded him. "No one can stop us now."

Without warning, Holden turned and shot Crane point-blank in the chest. Alyssa bit back a scream and turned away from the horrific sight.

"Easy," Gage murmured, so close she could feel his arm brushing against hers. Bile rose in her throat and she fought the urge to be sick.

"Idiot," Jefferson growled. "We're not far enough from shore to dump the body."

"He'll keep," Holden said, as if he hadn't just murdered a man in cold blood. "You know as well as I do, his boss was starting to get suspicious with all the hours Crane put in. Better to get rid of him now, before he could take any of us down with him."

"You still should have waited until we were farther out," Jefferson admonished him. "We can't afford to have bodies floating around too soon."

Alyssa knew, in that moment, that she and Gage would be next. A strange sense of calm came over her. She believed in God and if she died this afternoon, she knew she'd ultimately end up in a better place. And so would Gage. They'd be together in heaven.

Gage's warm hand touched hers, and she grasped it as if it were a lifeline. He'd come for her, just as she'd known he would. He might be stubborn and overprotective, but she wished now she'd told him how much she loved him.

She shifted slightly and saw the bottle of Scotch Jefferson had opened sitting on top of the bar. Gage met her gaze and gave a nearly imperceptible nod as he slid his hand into his pocket. He still had the pocketknife. A hysterical laugh threatened to bubble up from her chest. A half-empty bottle of Scotch and a pocketknife to defend themselves against two men with guns? What were they thinking? But then again, they also had faith and God on their side.

"So what do you think? They're too young to use the fake heart attack ploy," Holden was saying. "But maybe alcohol? They came on board to celebrate my win, drank too much and fell overboard?"

"Your army medic training is very handy," Jefferson mused in admiration. "Sure, why not? We'll claim we tried to find them but, alas, we couldn't."

Alyssa lifted her chin, refusing to let either Jefferson or Holden see any trace of fear. As sick and far-fetched as their plan was, she knew there were plenty of people willing to believe anything, especially the word of someone with money and prestige. Unfortunately, Jefferson and Holden had both.

How many lives had the two men taken? How many more before they were caught?

Gage's fingers brushed hers again, and he darted a glance out the side window, which was partially covered with horizontal blinds. Through the narrow slats, she saw lights from an approaching boat. Help on the way? By the way Gage's fingers pressed against hers, she thought for sure it was.

She glanced at him and easily read Gage's intention. Now was the time to make their move, especially since Holden had given Jefferson the gun so he could prepare a needle and syringe.

In a swift motion, she swept the bottle of Scotch off the bar and swung it at Holden's head, since he was closest to her. Thick glass met his even thicker skull, knocking the newly elected mayor off balance. Spinning around, she followed up with another well-aimed blow, knocking him to the floor. Alcohol spewed from the open end of the bottle, spraying over the walls and soaking into the soft carpet.

At the exact same moment, Gage rushed Jefferson, leading with the pocketknife but also going for the gun. A wild shot rang out and Alyssa ducked as pieces of the fancy chandelier overhead crashed down on them.

Sparks flew from the bulbs, and then flames sprouted like tiny, lethal fairies dancing madly along the alcohol-soaked carpet. Alyssa had knocked Holden unconscious, but she watched in horror as Gage and Jefferson wrestled for control of the gun.

Smoke gathered in the room, making her eyes water and obscuring her vision. She needed to help Gage, but how? The bottle she'd used on Holden rolled away, and she spent precious moments searching for it. But then she spied the silver blade of the knife. She grabbed it, gasping in pain as the heat from the metal burned her skin.

She wrapped part of her shirt around the knife handle and looked over to where Gage and Jefferson were rolling along the floor. Gage was on top of Jefferson, but they were dangerously close to the burning area of the carpeting. "Look out!" she cried. In a heartbeat, Jefferson rolled over on top of Gage, taking them farther from the fire.

What could she do to help Gage? The cord hanging off the horizontal blinds caught her eye and she used the knife to hack off a good-size section. Turning back to Jefferson and Gage, she was appalled to see Jefferson was on top of Gage, his hands around Gage's throat.

Moving fast, she darted forward and looped the string over Jefferson's head, pulling backward across his neck.

"Accckkkk," he gurgled, loosening his grip on Gage to grasp at his throat. Gage wrestled the gun out of the other man's grip and shot him.

Alyssa dropped the cord, watching in horror as Jefferson crumpled to the floor. The greedy flames had crawled up the walls, feeding off the interior of the yacht like a starving beast. They were almost completely surrounded by fire when she heard Gage shouting at her.

"Come on, let's go!" He grabbed her hand and dragged her through the narrow opening leading to the back of the yacht. Soon, they reached the small deck on the back of the boat.

The oncoming rescue boat was close, but not close enough. She heard a garbled sound behind them and glanced back in time to see a figure running toward them, waving his arms, clothes and hair on fire.

"Jump!" Gage shouted.

She jumped.

* * *

Shockingly cold water closed over his head. For a few moments he floated in the muffled silence, stunned at how fast the sharp, cold temperature numbed his limbs.

Alyssa! He struggled to kick his legs, propelling himself up to the surface. His strength faded fast, his movements sluggish. He had no idea how cold the water in Lake Michigan actually was, except to know it was too cold to stay immersed for long.

His head broke free, the air amazingly warm on his face. Gasping for breath, he looked frantically for Alyssa. The Coast Guard cutter moved steadily toward them, but where was Alyssa?

Panic swelled, making it harder to breathe. He knew she could swim, but where was she? Desperately, he turned in a circle, searching for a sign of her. He couldn't lose her now. He couldn't!

Not without telling her how much he loved her.

A flash of pink near the surface off to his right caught his eye and he forced his limbs into action, swimming as fast as he could.

"Alyssa!" he grabbed her supine body, dragging her face out of the water. With herculean strength, he flipped her over on her back.

She wasn't breathing!

"Gage! Alyssa!" He heard Jonah shouting at them from the Coast Guard cutter, but he couldn't respond. Alyssa was limp in his arms, and he cradled her head in the crook of his arm, bending over at an awkward angle to administer mouth-to-mouth breathing.

Again and again, he blew life-giving oxygen into her lungs, hoping, praying his feeble attempt would work. The Coast Guard boat came closer, and he willed her to hang on long enough to be rescued.

"Life preserver!" someone shouted from the side of the boat.

The circular life preserver at the end of a long line dropped beside him with a splash. He gave Alyssa one last, big breath before grabbing on.

She coughed and immediately threw up a lungful of lake water.

Thank You, Lord! Thank You!

"Ready!" Gage shouted. Within seconds, the Coast Guard drew them to safety, pulling Alyssa up first and then reaching down for him.

Several crew members must have noticed them shivering, because they were quickly wrapped in blankets.

"Jefferson?" Jonah asked, kneeling beside them.

He slowly shook his head. "I'm not sure if he's still on board or if he jumped into the water."

"He didn't jump," Jonah said with certainty. "We kept an eye on him, because if he had gotten overboard, we would have tried to save him. But he collapsed on the back deck and didn't move. They're going to try putting the fire out before taking the risk to board the boat."

Gage didn't blame them. He closed his eyes, silently begging God's forgiveness. He hadn't wanted to kill the guy. All he wanted was to escape long enough to get Alyssa out of there.

"Gage?" Alyssa's voice pulled him from his thoughts.

He glanced over at her and then reached out to pull her into his arms. Jonah backed off to give them privacy. "I'm sorry, Alyssa. I'm so sorry I left you alone at the motel."

"Shh, it's okay." She clung to him, burrowing close. "It's over. We're finally safe."

"Do you think God will forgive me?" he asked in a low, agonized tone. "I wasn't trying to kill him. I aimed the gun low, hoping to wound him. But then the fire..." He couldn't finish. The vision of the burning man would haunt him forever.

"Yes, Gage, I'm sure God will forgive both of us. God forgives all sins." She glanced back to where the burning boat still bobbed on the water. "Even theirs," she whispered.

"I never should have left you alone," he said again. "You were right, Alyssa. I'm sorry I've been so overprotective."

She pulled away to meet his gaze. "Why, Gage? What made you so overprotective?"

She'd never asked that before, and humbly he realized he should have talked about his past sooner. "My mother divorced my father when I was young, and she married a man who liked to use his fists. One night, their fighting woke me up and he was beating her, bad. I tried to stop him, but I was only ten and skinny as a rail. He leveled me with one blow. I dragged myself up and out of the house to get help, but I was too late. My mother suffered severe brain damage. She went into a coma and never woke up. She died three weeks later."

"Oh Gage," Alyssa murmured, wrapping her arms around him. "You should have told me."

She was right. There were so many things he should have done differently. Most important, he should have done a better job of embracing his faith. "I don't blame you for breaking off our engagement," he admitted. "I didn't take my relationship with God seriously, the way I should have. Now I can see that part of the reason was that I was still angry with Him, for taking my mother's life. In hindsight, I can see how I rationalized my need to work as more important than attending your study group." Suddenly, his less than stellar actions were crystal clear. "I only hope you'll let me attend your Bible study group again moving forward, so I can learn how to better serve God." He forced a smile. "Maybe once I graduate, you'll consider giving our relationship a second chance."

"Oh Gage," she murmured. "Of course I will." Before she could say anything more, Jonah returned.

"Sorry to interrupt, but the Coast Guard managed to put out the fire on Jefferson's yacht. Unfortunately, the only survivor was the guy driving the boat, who claims he doesn't know anything. Jefferson, Holden and Crane are all dead."

Guilt lodged in the back of his throat. If only he'd listened to Alyssa and taken her along. "I'm sorry."

Jonah's grim expression didn't help ease his guilt. "Unfortunately, we can't question them, to find out who they were working for."

Alyssa shifted in his arms, gaping at Jonah in shock. "You're right! Holden mentioned a boss. How did you know Jefferson wasn't the top guy?"

Jonah shrugged. "When I saw Crane dragging you onto the boat, I called my boss, who confided that they've suspected there were a couple of leaks in the department." He scowled, clearly upset with the thought of other dirty cops. "And then Rafe DeSilva mentioned they've been watching Jefferson's yacht for a long time, especially since he used the yacht often to go between Chicago and Milwaukee. They've seen Jefferson with several other men, one in particular who seemed to be the one in charge. Based on these two new pieces of information, they really wanted to take these guys alive."

"That's it!" Alyssa gripped Gage's arm. "Mallory isn't dead! Jefferson tried to get me to tell him where she was, so he obviously doesn't have her stashed away somewhere. Remember what you said, about Mallory taking off and hiding if she thought she was the target? I think you're right. She might have information about the guy in charge. We have to find her."

"Don't worry, finding Mallory has just risen to the top of my priority list," Jonah said, his tone lined with steely conviction. "My boss has given me the okay to continue working this case. For now, we're going to head back to shore."

When Jonah moved away, Gage glanced down at Alyssa. "I'll help find her, too," he vowed. "No matter what it takes, we'll bring her back, safe and sound."

"I know." When she smiled at him, his heart filled with joy. "I love you, Gage. I'm so thankful God watched over us and protected us."

He was humbled by her declaration, one he wasn't even sure he deserved. "I love you, too, Alyssa. More than you'll ever know. And I promise this time, I'll make you happy."

She hugged him hard and kissed him. *Thank You, Lord!* He silently rejoiced, knowing that accepting his faith had brought Alyssa home to him.

EPILOGUE

Alyssa used her new crutches to walk into Gage's house, where Jonah had already set up a satellite office. She was exhausted after spending the past few hours in the emergency department at Trinity Medical Center. Her face still burned with embarrassment at being poked and prodded by her colleagues. Using the crutches had also given her a new appreciation for the importance of upper-arm strength.

"Well?" Jonah asked, glancing up from his laptop computer. "I see they didn't keep you overnight."

"No, but she's going to have to come back," Gage said. "The orthopedic surgeon told her to stay off it for the next four to five days and then return for an MRI. He also told her he'd likely have to do surgery to repair the damage to her tendons and ligaments."

"But other than my ankle, I'm fine," she reminded him. "You saved my life, Gage. Minor repairs to my ankle are nothing in the big scheme of things." Gage had hovered over her gurney during the entire E.R. visit, and she knew he was still wrestling with guilt. She crutch-walked over to the sofa, and before she could even lift her foot off the floor, Gage was there to do it for her, putting her injured ankle up on a pillow. "Thanks," she murmured. She captured his hand in hers, gazing up at him, letting him see the love reflected in her eyes.

"Alyssa, who is Henry Stein?" Jonah asked abruptly. "Not Mallory's boyfriend, I hope."

She tore her gaze from Gage, belatedly remembering the glossy photo of Mallory and a strange man she'd found in the condo. Now that she had her memory, she vaguely remembered her twin was dating some guy named Anthony. "Don't be silly. Henry Stein is Uncle Henry. Well, actually, he's technically not our uncle; he's my mother's cousin. He must be in his late sixties or early seventies by now. Why are you asking about Uncle Henry?"

"Did you know he has a small lake cabin in Crystal Lake, Wisconsin?" Jonah asked.

"Oh, yeah, I guess now that you mention it, I do remember that," she mused. "Mallory and I went there a couple of times as kids. But I doubt Uncle Henry gets up there much anymore, though. He had a minor stroke last year and his left side is a little weaker than his right."

"So Mallory knew about the cabin."

"Yes." She smacked herself on the forehead. "I should have thought of the cabin sooner. Although to be honest, the cabin doesn't have the comforts of a hotel. It's a bit rough. And Mallory isn't the roughing-it kind of girl."

"Maybe not, but it's a lead I intend to follow up on," Jonah said as he shut down the computer. "I'm going to head up there tonight. If I find anything, I'll get in touch with you."

She glanced questioningly at Gage, who nodded. "Alyssa, you need to stay off that foot and get some rest. You trust Jonah, don't you?"

"Yes. Of course I trust Jonah." She smiled at Gage's best friend. "But promise me you'll call as soon as you know anything."

"I will. Take care, Alyssa. Gage." Jonah didn't waste any time. He slid the laptop into its carrying case and then headed for the door. Gage followed him out and then disappeared into the bedroom for several long minutes.

The house seemed eerily silent after Jonah left. Alyssa relaxed against the sofa cushions, reveling in the feeling of being safe at last. Gage returned about ten minutes later and came over to sit beside her on the sofa.

"Alyssa, did you mean what you said back on the boat?" he asked hesitantly.

"Yes, Gage." She knew exactly what he was trying to say. "I love you. And I believe you've deepened your relationship with God."

"I have, Alyssa. And I love you, too." He opened his palm and she saw her old engagement ring. "I can buy you a different one if you'd rather," he said quickly, when all she could do was stare in shock. "Will you do me the honor of being my wife?"

"Oh Gage," she murmured, holding out her left hand so he could slide her ring back on her finger, where it belonged. "Of course I'll marry you."

"I love you, Alyssa. More than I can ever say."

The modest diamond winked on her hand, and when Gage drew her carefully into his embrace, she knew this time, with the power of God's love, they'd make their relationship work.

* * * * *

Look for Jonah and Mallory's story,
TWIN PERIL, by Laura Scott,
available August 2012
from Love Inspired Suspense.

Dear Reader,

I've always been fascinated by twins, especially identical twins. I've seen TV documentaries about twins separated at birth who have the same careers, the same medical problems, even the same hobbies. But what if you had identical twins with completely different personalities? This sparked the idea for my next two stories.

Alyssa and Mallory are twins, but due to a traumatic event when Mallory was younger, they lead very different lifestyles—until danger forces them to take each other's personalities.

Gage Drummond was engaged to Alyssa Roth, but after a few short months, she gave him his ring back because he was overprotective and didn't have a close relationship with God. But when Alyssa is in danger, he's willing to risk his life to save hers.

Reunited love is the theme of *Identity Crisis* in Alyssa and Gage's story. And stay tuned for the sequel, Mallory and Jonah's story, TWIN PERIL. I'm always thrilled to hear from my readers, and I can be reached through my website at wwww.laurascottbooks.com.

Yours in faith,
Laura Scott

Questions for Discussion

1. In the beginning of the story, Alyssa is overwhelmed with guilt because she feels she caused her twin's death. Have you ever felt guilty for hurting someone you love? Please discuss.

2. Gage agrees to pick up Mallory at the hospital to help get into Alyssa's good graces. Was that a good reason? Why or why not?

3. We learn Gage has a deep fear of failure when it comes to protecting the ones he loves. Have you had to cope with a similar failure? Please discuss.

4. Alyssa has amnesia and believes she's Mallory, but she doesn't feel comfortable in her own home. Do you think having amnesia can change your basic personality? Why or why not?

5. Gage discovers Alyssa's true identity, but Alyssa isn't ready to believe him. Did you understand her reluctance? Why or why not?

6. At one point in the story, Gage begins to renew his faith for real, not just because

Alyssa asked him to. Discuss a moment in your life when you renewed your faith.

7. Do you think Bible study will help Gage become closer to God? Please discuss.

8. At one point in the story, Alyssa had to stitch up a deep cut in Gage's wrist. Describe a time when you had to hurt someone you loved in order to help them.

9. Alyssa regains her memory and remembers everything, including breaking up with Gage. Yet she is also willing to give him a second chance. Do you think this is a good idea? Why or why not?

10. Alyssa was upset when Gage didn't treat her as an equal partner in their relationship. Did you agree with her feelings? Why or why not?

11. Toward the end of the story, Gage killed a man in self-defense. Do you think God will forgive him? Why or why not?

12. Gage and Alyssa's story is a reunion story. Do you like reunion stories? Why or why not?

LARGER-PRINT BOOKS!

**GET 2 FREE
LARGER-PRINT NOVELS
PLUS 2 FREE
MYSTERY GIFTS**

Love Inspired®

Larger-print novels are now available...

YES! Please send me 2 FREE LARGER-PRINT Love Inspired® novels and my 2 FREE mystery gifts (gifts are worth about $10). After receiving them, if I don't wish to receive any more books, I can return the shipping statement marked "cancel". If I don't cancel, I will receive 6 brand-new novels every month and be billed just $4.99 per book in the U.S. or $5.49 per book in Canada. That's a saving of at least 23% off the cover price. It's quite a bargain! Shipping and handling is just 50¢ per book in the U.S. and 75¢ per book in Canada.* I understand that accepting the 2 free books and gifts places me under no obligation to buy anything. I can always return a shipment and cancel at any time. Even if I never buy another book, the two free books and gifts are mine to keep forever.

122/322 IDN FEG3

Name _____ (PLEASE PRINT)

Address _____ Apt. #

City _____ State/Prov. _____ Zip/Postal Code

Signature (if under 18, a parent or guardian must sign)

Mail to the **Reader Service:**

IN U.S.A.: P.O. Box 1867, Buffalo, NY 14240-1867
IN CANADA: P.O. Box 609, Fort Erie, Ontario L2A 5X3

Not valid to current subscribers to Love Inspired Larger-Print books.

**Are you a current subscriber to Love Inspired books
and want to receive the larger-print edition?
Call 1-800-873-8635 or visit www.ReaderService.com.**

* Terms and prices subject to change without notice. Prices do not include applicable taxes. Sales tax applicable in N.Y. Canadian residents will be charged applicable taxes. Offer not valid in Quebec. This offer is limited to one order per household. All orders subject to credit approval. Credit or debit balances in a customer's account(s) may be offset by any other outstanding balance owed by or to the customer. Please allow 4 to 6 weeks for delivery. Offer available while quantities last.

Your Privacy—The Reader Service is committed to protecting your privacy. Our Privacy Policy is available online at www.ReaderService.com or upon request from the Reader Service.

We make a portion of our mailing list available to reputable third parties that offer products we believe may interest you. If you prefer that we not exchange your name with third parties, or if you wish to clarify or modify your communication preferences, please visit us at www.ReaderService.com/consumerchoice or write to us at Reader Service Preference Service, P.O. Box 9062, Buffalo, NY 14269. Include your complete name and address.

LILP11B